SHADOW DANCERS

LEVI GALLUP

DIVERTIR
PUBLISHING
Salem, NH

SHADOW DANCERS

LEVI GALLUP

Cover design by Rich Normandin

Published by Divertir Publishing LLC
PO Box 232
North Salem, NH 03073
http://www.divertirpublishing.com/

ISBN-13: 978-1-938888-02-1
ISBN-10: 1-938888-02-2

Library of Congress Control Number: 2013935017

Printed in the United States of America

Dedication

This book is dedicated to those who've passed before us, their unfulfilled aspirations yet lingering in their hearts, and to the hope that in rebirth they have achieved them.

Contents

Prologue

People have a hard time believing in anything supernatural, but the denial of its existence has no affect on its existence. In reality, it is the essence of our being. All around us the world is alive with signals, with impulses, with data. Most people have traded the ability to perceive these signals for the security of an ego, but just like radio waves, x-rays, and infrared, they are very much there. Some people are quite attuned while others are unable to perceive even the slightest hint that there is more to this world than what we can see, touch, taste, smell and hear. A multitude of people tread somewhere in between.

Multiverse theory suggests that you and I exist in multiple dimensions. Even as you read this, another incarnation of "you" is sleeping, eating, dying, giving birth, or having sex. These alternate realities can exist at any moment in time and indicate that time is not truly linear but cyclical. At any moment, we exist in the past, present and future. Often we are granted a vision of these 'other lives' in dreams or in fleeting moments of enlightenment. Sometimes these virtual expressions bring joy, peace, and wisdom. Other times they bring fear, heartache, and suffering.

There are stories told where such encounters prove to be a dire warning, a warning that immediate events are compounded upon the past or a warning of vengeful spirits on the loose and of impending doom. Sometimes the shadows of other realities cross into our own, and when they do... untold havoc can be unleashed and demons released upon the unsuspecting. This is one such story.

The Letter

Dear Friend,   September 6th…

I reckon it seems insane that I'm pausing long enough to scribble this letter because it may just cost me my life. But I'm determined that others be warned about what I've witnessed, so I'm pursuing this in hopes of making you aware of what has happened here over the past few days. As I write this it's fixin' to get real bad 'round here.

I'm sending this to you because in the event things continue to go sour I want my journal in the hands of someone who might actually believe in its contents and be willing to tell others.

I have recorded in my journal most of what has gone on which, if you have received this note, is now in your possession. When I started writing I wasn't quite sure where to begin, so I started it where I first remembered things going off in this direction.

Please don't think poorly of me or think all the gray matter has leaked out of my brainpan; I've already considered those things myself. Just know that what I have written in this journal happened, and what is happening right now is as real as it gets. And the next time you witness a whirlwind… Well just remember what you've learned here.

I hope I get to share this with you in person and to share it with as many people as possible, but things aren't looking too good right now. It seems all hell is fixin' to break loose.

Be well my friend,
Brady

Journal entry: August 29, 10:02 p.m. Things got weird today. And I mean real weird.

※ 1 ※

Brake! Brakesy! Get over here and sit down, you damn redneck."

I released the door allowing it to close behind me, the string of metallic bells strung across its top edge jingling as the door swung shut. The sound caused the other diners to glance up at me momentarily distracted from their breakfasts. Seated around metallic, stainless steel tables or along the ceramic topped bar running the length of the diner most nodded an acknowledgment before returning their attention to their food or coffee.

Tearing my eyes away from the shapely form of Jennie Marshall as she reached to pull down a package of paper napkins from atop a cabinet, I worked my way along the row of booths at the front of the Dustbowl Diner then veered toward the middle of the room. The diner, its interior cast in the cold, hard chrome, glass, Formica, and red vinyl décor of the 1950s era, was full of nostalgic charm. The warmth of staff and patrons was welcoming to anyone who ventured inside, and it was a familiar place for me to meet my friends. My hungry stomach growled in response to the pleasing aromas of numerous steaming plates of eggs, bacon, home fries, and toast. I grasped the vinyl cushioned back of the one vacant chair at the table where Billy Don Smith, Jimmy Joe Jackson, and Bobby 'Red' McCauley sat forking eggs and bacon into their mouths between a constant flow of words and coffee.

"Where the hell you been this morning? I thought maybe you'd gone home with that sweet little Missy Briggs last night," Billy Don chortled. He sported a broad grin, his white teeth made brighter by the contrast of two days' growth of dark whiskers along his narrow jaw. His eyes twinkled behind thick eyeglasses, and his graying black hair grew thick beneath his dusty black Stetson. A notepad and pencil protruded from the left pocket of his gray, western-style shirt. The rest of us wore logo emblazoned work shirts and ball caps paired with cowboy boots, denim jeans, and large, silver belt buckles. Billy's polished silver buckle sported an oil rig, longhorn cattle, a five-pointed star, and the word *Texas*.

Before I could respond Betty Jane Wilcox strode up to the table with a steaming hot pot of coffee. She grabbed up the overturned ceramic cup from the saucer in front of me just as I settled into the chair. Betty was a slender little gal with a full bosom, narrow waist and contoured hips covered in an apron that made all the boys' eyes follow her as she walked.

"Mornin', Brake. Coffee?" Betty asked, pursing her ruby red lips and winking one of her mascara-painted eyes.

Billy Don watched my eyes as I ogled the girl—something I did out of reflex more than actual interest. Not wanting to be left out he sat up straight and leaned forward.

"You're lookin' mighty sweet this morning, Betty Jane. How about bendin' over in front of me and pourin' a cup of your *fine* coffee." Billy Don clicked his tongue, winking in a flirtatious manner.

Betty poured coffee into my cup without waiting for my response and looked directly at Billy Don. "You hush your fresh mouth in here, Billy Don. You're too old to be talking like that."

"Too old? Hell, you come right on over here, honey, and sit on my lap. I'll show how old I am."

"You old geezer. You know you can't cut the mustard no more." She curtsied, winking at me as she refilled Red's cup.

"I might be too old to cut the mustard, Betty Jane, but I'm still damn good at lickin' the jar!" His comment caused a burst of laughter to erupt from the many truckers and oil rig roughnecks sitting in the roadside diner. Betty Jane scampered back toward the kitchen blushing and giggling nervously.

When the laughter died down I answered Billy. "No, I went home right after you boys left the Cactus Creek last night." I was referring to the saloon we all used as a watering hole after work most nights. Sipping my coffee, I reached up and adjusted the dirty ball cap atop my head. "What's on tap for today?"

Bobbie Sue Bennett, an older woman but easy to look at with her brunette locks tied up in a ponytail, and sporting her own shapely figure, approached the table giving an embarrassed Betty Jane a moment to collect herself.

"Good Morning, you bunch of wranglers. We got a chicken-fried steak with gravy and hash browns and a blueberry and ice cream waffle for specials. What's it gonna be this morning, Brady?"

"I'll stick with the ham and bacon omelet with extra onion, Texas toast, and home fries."

"Okay, honey. You want juice or anything with that?"

"Yeah, I'll have me an orange juice."

"You got it, handsome," she said, spinning away from the table and whacking Billy Don on the shoulder with the menu as she walked past him and continued toward the kitchen. "Ya'll behave yourselves out here."

Billy Don chuckled, satisfied that he had drawn enough attention to himself, and looked up at me. He pulled out the pad of paper, glanced at it briefly, and pushed it back into the Western cut pocket. His gaze returned to me as he picked up his coffee cup and took a long swallow before returning the cup to its saucer. "I need you to go out to the Snodgrass, Barbara George, and Henderson/Crabtree leases today, Brake. If that don't take you all day give me a shout on the horn, and I'll find you another."

Brake. I got the name fresh out of high school. Billy Don taught me just about everything I know about truck driving and hauling crude oil. When I was first learning to drive a truck I came up on a stop sign a little too quickly and Billy hollered at me. "Goddamn it, Brady, brake! Hit the drake, Brake!" He meant to say, "Hit the brake, Drake," but where my first name is Brady and last name Drake… Then he got to tellin' the other guys about the incident… You know how it goes. Everyone picked up on it, and since then he calls me Brake as do the others on occasion.

"Okay," I said. "That works fine for me."

Over some friendly banter we sipped our coffees, finished eating breakfast, and paid our tabs before leaving the restaurant. Just as I was about to climb up into the cab of my truck, J.J. Jackson, a life-long friend and neighbor of mine, hollered to me. I waited for him as he walked over to my rig: a sparkling and well-maintained eighteen-wheeled tanker and tractor.

"Brake, you mind swappin' one of your leases with me? I've got to pick up Felicia over in Sundown after work, and it would be a whole lot better for me if I could finish the day runnin' over to the George lease. Since you're goin' out toward New Mexico anyway I thought maybe you could do the Hobgoode lease. They pay 'bout the same. Besides, you know how you like those burritos at Taos Taco in Morton, so you'd be able to stop in and get a couple if ya' had a mind to."

"Okay, J.J., so you'll be runnin' over to the Barbara George then?"

"Yeah."

"Sure, no problem."

"Great! Thanks, Brady."

With a nod, J.J. spun around on his heels and jogged off toward his rig. I climbed up into mine and settled in.

J.J. had been born in the Flats just west of Levelland, but he and his folks moved to Broken Spoke when he was eight years old so his mama could work in the cotton gin. His first day in school a group of boys from the outer farms picked on him. They called him some nasty, racist shit and took to roughin' him up.

My buddy Eddie and I jumped to his side of things, and after givin' them other boys a thrashin' we've all been friends ever since. Both J.J. and I had a crush on a brown-eyed gal by the name of Felicia, but I was too interested in playing the field, and he was full in love with the girl. Good thing because they've been together since high school, and I still haven't settled down. He's a good man and great friend.

Having left the semi running while I was inside, the diesel engine was warmed up and ready to roll. I released the air brakes on the truck and tanker and slid the lever into first gear. As I released the clutch, the massive machine rattled, hummed, and roared, and I was soon rolling along Route 114, headed west toward Whiteface.

Tuning the radio to a country station, I started humming along to the newest song from Rascal Flats. With the sun rising steadily into the clear, blue Texas sky the cool morning air was beginning to warm, and it was shaping up to be a right gorgeous day. Forty minutes passed before I pulled up alongside the storage tanks on the Snodgrass oil lease. Jackrabbits scurried through the underbrush, the rattle of the truck putting a scare into them. The pump jack, a monster of a pump handle sliding up and down atop a concrete slab in the ground, was humming and creaking—pumping that Texas tea out of the ground and into the pair of five-hundred barrel storage tanks. The odor of crude oil was thick in the air. It's an ever-present scent in the panhandle of Texas but noticeably more pungent the nearer to a lease tank you find yourself.

Hopping down out of the cab, I lifted the lid on my toolbox and grabbed my test kit. I climbed up the ladder on the first tank and hooked the kit on a rung just in front of me. I released the lever on the tank hatch and leaned away from the lid and slowly lifted it open. The tank spewed the vile fumes of the pure Texas crude as I let it rest in an angled position.

As I lowered a sample container down into the oil, visions from a training video raced through my head: images of men who had opened the lids without leaning back and were killed by the toxic gas escaping the tank. You'd think that, since I perform this task eighteen to twenty times a week, I'd forget about those images, but they show the same damn video every year during the annual safety training courses. We get the pleasure of seeing it again and again, and I sure as hell don't want to end up like any of them. If I did I guess someone would take snapshots of me and use them to put a scare into other haulers. Personally, I feel it would be damn disgraceful if somebody found my corpse hanging on the ladder or in a heap on the ground below it.

Ugh, not for me.

Drawing my sample up out of the tank, I filled a couple of test tubes, put them back in their holders, and popped a cap on them. Then I closed the lid, grabbed my kit, climbed down the ladder, and returned to the truck. I put the test kit back in the toolbox and slipped the two test tubes into the spinner and turned it on. As the tubes spun they separated the water, oil, and sediments inside.

A few minutes later the test was complete and the oil passed the purchase criteria. I wrestled the hose from the side of the truck and hooked it up to the tank before I started the pump. The smelly, black crude poured into the tanker while I wrote out a purchase tag to leave in the receipt box.

Half an hour later I was back on the road and heading southeast to dump the load at a central pumping station. Once there, I off-loaded the crude into a massive storage tank and headed on out to another lease to repeat the task. As to the crude oil, well, it gets pumped out from the pump station through a series of underground pipes and will make its way to a regional oil refinery.

The rest of my day went something like that. As I said, it was a damn fine day and payday to boot. Last run of the day was the Hobgoode lease, a desolate spot out near the New Mexico border. It was after four o'clock by the time I got the crude loaded into the tanker. I secured the hoses before climbing back into the truck. I then turned the old Mack tractor east and headed for my last trip to Brownfield station.

I barreled down a long stretch of barren highway, the pumping station drawing ever closer, as the miles passed beneath my wheels. Soon, I approached the desolate fork in the road known as Ten Mile Fork. Gazing out on the few old, run-down buildings and a rusted Texaco sign I noticed a handmade placard mounted under the star advertising a recently opened convenience store. Suddenly, I had a strong hankering for something cold to drink. My thermos full of iced coffee had long since been drained, and there wasn't another store between here and Brownfield pumping station. I pulled in and parked alongside the edge of the road just twenty feet from the antique gas pumps. The outdated pumps still provided gasoline, but the office section of the garage had been converted into the miniature convenience store. The open automotive bays no longer served their original purpose and were now filled with junk. Except for a few outbuildings around the station and an old farmhouse across the street nothing but crop fields and a few stands of trees was visible through the windows of the cab.

Hot air engulfed me as I opened the door and stepped down onto the hard-packed, reddish brown earth. Walking away from the truck, I raised my ball cap and wiped the sweat from my brow as I squinted against the wind, blocking out the dust it was carrying across the open prairie.

The whir of an old air conditioner buzzed above my head, and a drop of water falling from the sweating metal struck my shoulder as I reached for the doorknob. When I stepped inside I discovered that the air wasn't much cooler, but it was an improvement.

The old place smelled of fuel, oil and stale coffee. Racks of gray, metal shelving stood in the center of the concrete floor holding a limited selection of canned goods and packaged foodstuffs. A glass-topped cooler with a small selection of ice cream products hummed loudly near the front window, and several drink coolers lined the back wall of the small room. A rugged metal counter ran along one wall behind which a clerk stood in front of several racks of cigarettes. The walls were devoid of decoration but for a few ancient fan belts and a yellowed calendar, dated 1969, with a photograph of an antique Ford pickup truck.

The last year they made any improvements here, I thought as I approached one of the coolers. The selection was pretty small, so I settled for grabbing a Yoohoo from the buzzing refrigerator and crossed the room to the counter where I paid the old man. He didn't say a word until he handed back my change.

"Breeze don't seem to be coolin' things down none, does it?" the lanky, gray haired clerk remarked glancing at me over the reading spectacles resting on the bridge of his nose.

"Nah, too damn hot," I agreed. "Thanks." I tilted my face away from the rancid, tobacco-dip laced breath that assaulted my nostrils as he spoke.

"Still says a hundred and three there on the thermometer outside the window," he said, seemingly reluctant to allow our conversation to end.

"Yeah, that seems about right." I turned away and headed for the door.

"Ya'll come on back, now." The old man returned his gaze to a sportsman magazine laid out on the counter.

Nodding, I stepped out through the door and pulled it closed behind me. Once again, the heat wrapped around my body and made me think immediately of the air-conditioned haven waiting inside the cab of my truck. I cracked the top on the Yoohoo bottle and flicked the bottle cap into an open fifty-gallon trash drum before taking a long swig of the ice-cold, chocolate-flavored mixture. Savoring the liquid as it flooded my mouth and ran down my throat, I scanned the immediate landscape.

An old pickup truck, which didn't look as though it had run in years, sat rusting away near the aged Texaco signpost. But for the fuel pumps, an old shack, another late model pickup that had seen better days, and several scrap piles, not much else littered the grounds. Around the station were unplanted fields waiting their turn in the crop rotation cycle. The bare dirt was dry, and little puffs of dust wafted in ghostly formations just above the ground until they fell once again to the earth. In all directions the land lay flat all the way to the horizon. Here and there an occasional tree, or group of trees, sprouted up from the earth shading some small portion of the sun-baked land. That was all that managed to eke out a living in this desolate place. Some of the fields at the far reaches of my vision sported cotton. Their irrigation pipes spanned acres of land, and lush, green plants struggled daily in their ever-reaching quest toward the sky. Few clouds dared enter the blue afternoon sky over Texas. It was a domain occupied only by the large, yellow sun as it glared down at the earth, baking the ancient soil with its gaze.

I wiped away a smudge of chocolate from my upper lip with my sleeve, and as I lifted my head I noticed a woman. She stepped away from the side of the building and strode across the lot toward the old signpost. My eyes were drawn immediately to her slender legs which began at the barely visible curve in her shapely buttocks, encased in tight blue shorts, and gleamed all the way down to the tops of her leather boots. I immediately sized her up to be about thirty-five years old. Dirty-blond hair fell down around her partially-naked shoulders, exposed by the cut of her lime green blouse. With the bottom of her shirt rolled up and tied in a knot just below her bosom the unbuttoned top exposed much of her ample breasts as she worked. Her body held my attention as she reached up to change the fuel price placards on the sign.

I stared for a moment too long before looking away suspecting she had spotted my roving eyes. When I risked a second glance at her cleavage she knowingly met my gaze. I grinned offering her a nervous nod. The woman winked at me and blew me a little kiss making me feel all the more uncomfortable.

As she turned her back to me, her attention returning to the task at hand, I thought she cocked her buttocks just a *bit* higher than necessary as she lifted one leg and then rose up onto the concrete base to reach the higher placards. As the wind tossed her hair about her pleasant face she moved around to the other side of the sign. Once again, the woman caught me staring at her, and I was pleased to note her eyes roving over me as well. I nodded again. No longer uneasy, I openly enjoyed the sight of her. While watching glistening sweat rising on her creamy skin I began musing over the idea of maybe taking a turn at her if she was of a mind to do so.

As I tipped back the bottle for the last of the Yoohoo I noticed a whirling mass of sand headed in the direction of the signpost. I watched with some amusement as the dust devil approached the woman. She was completely unaware of the twirling dust as she dutifully worked at finishing her task.

Amused, I watched more intently, wondering what effect the wind might have on her flimsy blouse. I tossed the empty bottle into the open steel drum near the door and stepped away from the building as I sauntered in her direction. Heck, I figured the potential rescue of a damsel in distress might be worthy of some reward.

The whirlwind whipped the woman's hair about her head and tugged at her top. Startled, she dropped the placards and moved away from the sign, attempting to escape the sand blasting her exposed skin. I felt a sudden sinking feeling in my gut when the whirlwind seemed to move with her, and my amusement became full-fledged uneasiness.

The wind intensified, and the women seemed as though she were paralyzed in its grasp. Her eyes sought mine and, as our gazes collided, I could read the fear in her green eyes. I jogged toward her now truly intent on rescuing her. All playful thoughts of a reward for my gallant rescue evaporated in the face of her genuine terror. But before I could reach her I lost sight of her as the sand in the miniature tornado swallowed the woman completely. The swirling tempest began to roar around her, and particles of sand pelted my face. I lifted my arms to protect my skin and squinted my eyes. Startled by the sheer force of the whirlwind, I stumbled backward while resisting its attempt to engulf me as well.

A ghastly hissing and gurgling noise followed by a sickly sound of bones popping erupted from the swirling mass of sand. The green blouse, shredded with parts of it missing, was flung from the whirlwind along with a boot and a bracelet. I began to shake. Weakness flooded me, and I felt lightheaded as sweat sprang from my pores, and my heart began to pound in my chest. I retraced my steps, retreating toward the store with the hair on the back of my neck standing on end. What happened next will stick with me for the rest of my days.

I stared at the aftermath of the bizarre event for a moment before I ground my fists into my eye sockets and blinked rapidly in an attempt to refocus. I couldn't believe my eyes. Awe was replaced by a sense of foreboding, and then fear that gripped me unlike anytime ever in my life. I felt flush, my breathing becoming difficult, as I staggered backward with my mind reeling.

Appearing from what remained of the spinning sand was a man. He was dark-skinned, muscular in a sinewy kind of way, and naked but for some kind of amulet hanging around his neck. He staggered out of the whirlwind, seemingly in pain, and the miniature tornado swept off across the parking lot and faded away. Still unbelieving, I looked for the woman who no longer seemed to exist, and stared into the enlarged, haunting, eyes the depth of which seemed eternal and demonic. He stared at me, his gaze boring through me as if searching for my soul.

Stumbling backwards, I tripped and slammed my back against the front door as I fumbled for the doorknob. The door seemed to vanish when I gripped the knob and turned. It sprung open from the force of my body, and I found myself falling backward. I flailed, struggling to remain upright, while accidentally raking a row of canned goods off the shelf with my right arm. Gasping for breath, I lost my bid to remain on my feet and found myself sprawling on my back across the concrete floor inside. I scooted further toward the rear of the store and away from the doorway clawing for anything that might help me right myself.

"What the hell is going on?" squawked the old store clerk. "Close the damn door before the wind blows sand all up in here."

Finding a support beam, I pulled myself to my feet but continued to back away from the door while seeking the whereabouts of the creature I had just seen manifest out of the whirlwind. I stared out through the large plate glass window and located the creature as it crossed in front of the building. His rugged facial features and long, black mane made me wonder if he was of American Indian or Mexican blood, but my mind was far too distracted to really spend much time thinking about it. Despite his forceful gait the man seemed slightly disoriented as he approached the front of the establishment with an increasing sense of intensity in his movements.

"G—get…" I stammered, looking toward the aged store clerk. My vocal chords were taut, choked by the adrenaline coursing hot within my veins, and I found myself unable to continue my warning. Numb and awestruck, I stood motionless while I struggled to gather my thoughts. I felt paralyzed by the horror of what I had just witnessed.

"Get outta here!" I finally heard myself scream after numerous attempts as I frantically looked about for another way out of the store. At that moment the black-eyed creature stepped through the open doorway. His mouth opened, and the blood-curdling howl he unleashed sent ice cold shivers through my entire body.

"What in the hell do ya think your doin', boy? We don't allow no screaming, longhaired, shirtless hippies in here. Can't you read the sign? No shirt, no shoes, no service," the old man barked from behind the counter. "And where the *hell* are your goddamned pants?" The clerk's voice trembled as he backed away, cowering against the cigarettes.

The dark man turned his eyes on the aged clerk, his face still holding that vicious mask of rage. His muscles rippled and with lightning speed he snatched up a can of chili beans that I had managed not to knock onto the floor in my stumbling. The creature's arm whipped forward, and he heaved the can of beans square at the old man. Rocketing through the air as though it had been fired from an ancient cannon, the can struck the store clerk in the sternum with a resounding thud.

The old man grunted at the impact as he was flung backward into the cigarette cartons. He lurched sideways before disappearing, falling down behind the counter. The sound of items being strewn about under the counter filled my ears as I turned my focus back on the black-eyed monster. His gaze was already locked onto me, and a second can of chili beans missed cracking my skull by mere inches. Eyeing an interior door, the only other exit I saw, I ducked behind the shelves nearest me and scampered across the store.

"God-damned heathen!" The old man emerged from beneath the counter and pointed the barrel of a shotgun toward the unwelcome guest.

The gun roared just as I passed the end of the service counter and charged through the doorway. The shriek that erupted behind me made me hesitate and turn to look. *Did he get him?* I wondered.

Crouching, I crept back through the interior doorway, hoping to see that evil bastard dead. However I could only watch in terror as the heathen seemed to fly across the room and land atop the counter. The demon kicked the shotgun, and the old man fired again as it jerked upwards, blasting a hole in the ceiling. Concrete and paint rained down on the pair. Leaping off the counter, the creature wrapped his legs around the clerk's waist and plunged one of his thumbs deep into the other man's left eye socket. There was a sucking sound as the man's eyeball popped free, and he began to wail, dropping the shotgun entirely, as he clawed frantically at his own face.

I have never considered myself to be a coward, but I was in full panic mode and too damned near messing my pants to stop and play the hero. I bolted back through the doorway and into a cluttered stock room as the old man shrieked and cried for mercy behind me. From the sounds coming from that room I could only imagine the horrendous death the old timer was suffering at the hands of this murderous devil.

Tumbling over a stack of boxes and food cartons, I ran blindly seeking an exit. After a few minutes of panicked movement I noticed the side door and tore at it, slamming my body into the frame when it didn't open. Boy did I feel dumb when I spotted the latch on the old screen door. I pushed the latch down and fell forward, rolling across the dirt, before springing to my feet. As soon as I knew what direction was up I was running for my truck.

Halfway across the front lot I heard the bellow of the .20 gauge shotgun from behind me and felt the sting of birdshot as a partial load spattered my left arm and shoulder. The worst of it swept past me and collided with one of the antique fuel pumps. I turned and looked for him, and to my horror the dark-eyed devil was barreling through the front door of the store with the clerk's shotgun firmly in hand.

Dressed now in the old man's dirty denim pants, the devil looked almost human as he fired another shot in my direction but missed completely. His gaze remained fixed on me as he ejected the shells; it took him only a moment to reload. Turning the shotgun, he pointed the muzzle at a five gallon fuel can set next to a lawn mower in the open door of the garage. The can burst sending gasoline everywhere. I suspected then that those shells were loaded with steel shot because when the pellets struck the metal and brick inside the bay tiny sparks ignited the gasoline, and flames quickly spread across the garage interior.

He then sighted the weapon in on me once more. Spinning about, I dove and rolled across the dirt as the round tore out of the barrel. Fear of being shot again propelled me as I heard the sound of more birdshot ripping into the gas pumps behind where I had just been standing. My flight mechanism in full gear, I continued the dash for my truck. Once there I sprang up, grasped the door handle, and whipped open the door of the cab only to feel a strong hand slam into me. Claw like fingernails shredded my shirt and tore my skin as they raked down my lower back before the bony fingers curled around my belt and jerked me backwards.

I reached for the tire bar, reacting more than I was thinking, and somehow my hands found the Maglite I kept on the floor next to the seat. The flashlight fell from my fingers, and I rolled backwards as I struck the ground, coming up on my feet as the fiend lunged at me. His body struck mine with such force that we tumbled across the lot grabbing and punching at one another like feral cats fighting over territory. My fingers found an amulet, and I twisted the rawhide tether tightly around his neck. The heathen stopped trying to claw my eyes out and got to his feet, trying to get loose of my grip. Seemingly more annoyed than concerned, he wrenched himself away in a singular jerk. The cord snapped, and he staggered away from me as the pressure was abruptly released. I darted sideways and scrambled across the dirt, recovering the flashlight from where I'd dropped it. I managed to get myself up on one knee when he charged. Leaping directly at the charging monster, I swung the flashlight and, with a speed and accuracy that surprised me, clobbered him square in the temple. As the flashlight collided with the side of the man's skull the cylinder dented, lens popped off, and the batteries rocketed through the air. The demon slammed into the earth and rolled over amidst the rising dust with blood pouring from a gash just in front of his left ear. The distraction gave me just enough time to get back to the truck. Leaping up through the open door and into the cab I jerked the door closed, slapped the door lock with my elbow, and released the brakes. I jammed my foot down on the clutch and popped the transmission into gear. As the big rig heaved and began to move, I stared out at the store, fearing the bastard might already be on me. The heathen was still stunned, slowly pushing himself up from the dust and shaking his head. As I watched the rolling inferno inside the garage I prayed that he might be roasted in the flames.

Dumbstruck, I shifted the gears by instinct and drove, trying to escape the surreal event. As I put distance between myself and that *thing* my gaze returned repeatedly to the mirror. I watched in the mirror as the devil got to his feet and made his way across the yard. Approaching the front of the building, he grabbed up a chunk of burning debris and tossed it into the store. Then he stood still for a moment, watching my rig, watching me, before he turned away.

Every gained inch of ground between me and that God forsaken gas station was a moment of joy, but fear remained nestled low in my gut. I glanced again at the reflection of the station in the mirror and jumped in my seat, stunned by the sound of a horrendous explosion. I could only stare in disbelief at the fireball that erupted into the sky behind me. He had obviously set fire to the fuel pumps and the entire area was engulfed in a raging inferno. Billowing black smoke hovered in the hot afternoon air.

"Holy shit, what the hell was that thing?" I screamed, wiping sweat from my eyes and face using my left sleeve. Consciously working to calm myself, I began to take inventory of my injuries. I was well aware of the stinging slashes in my lower back where the fiend had scratched me, and I figured on at least a couple dozen pellets of birdshot were embedded in my upper back and shoulder. Quivering with sudden nervousness, I ran my hand over my sweaty face once again.

In that moment I became frightened all over again as I realized what I was holding. A tether was entwined in my fingers, and the fiend's amulet hung, swaying, just below my left wrist. Repulsed, I shook my hand violently and watched as the thing wriggled clear and flew across the interior of the cab. It landed on the floor though I wasn't exactly certain where. I made a mental note to ditch the thing as soon as I felt comfortable enough to stop. Pondering all that I had just witnessed and somehow survived, as well as considering my own possible insanity, I drove eastward.

 ❊ 2 ❊

Brake! What the hell's wrong with you? Your goddamn truck still has a load on!" Billy Don shouted as he entered the Cactus Creek Saloon and walked toward the barstool where I sat nursing a beer. His words startled me, shaking me as though I were waking from a dream, and interrupting the endless stream of images constantly replaying the events at Ten Mile Fork. Lost in thought and haunted by the memories of this afternoon, I came to the abrupt realization that I had driven right past Brownfield station and forgotten to dump the load.

"Shit, Billy, I'm sorry. I'll dump it before I go home."

"How many of them beers you had?" Hacking a dry cough, he lit and took the first drag on a fresh cigarette.

"First one. And I'll go when I'm done with it," I said defensively.

"What in the *hell* were you thinkin'?" Billy Don demanded as he hiked up onto the stool next to me and signaled the bartender with his finger that he'd take his usual: a shot of whiskey and a Coors draft.

"I wasn't thinkin'. I had a real bad time of it out in…" I whispered, as my voice just trailed off.

"Well, it don't look like you hit anything. Did you have a spill or somethin'?"

"No, no…" I said, not really wanting to talk about it. *Hell, he's going to think I'm crazy if I say anything.*

"Hey, Brake!" Red Macaulay sauntered into the air-conditioned saloon. "You takin' a load home with you tonight?"

"He had a run in with a jackrabbit, or a coyote, or something, and it's thrown him all off balance," Billy Don offered, chuckling as he glanced back at me. "Boy fuckin' howdy, Brake! Your shoulder's

21

bleeding, and you're all scratched up back here. Did you fall into some barbed wire or something?"

His chiding tone changed to concern as his hand swept upward in an attempt to get a look at my shoulder. "Hell, Brady, that looks like birdshot. What happened?"

"It weren't no fuckin' jackrabbit, or ladder, or barbed wire," I barked before he could finish speaking. I shrugged away from him, wincing and grabbing my mug of beer. As I turned to face the two men I wanted to tell them what I had seen. But in the next moment I thought better of offering anything more. Hell, *I* wasn't sure what I had seen, or if maybe I was losing it all together.

The worsening sting from the pellets in my shoulder and the scratches across my back and hip reminded me that I needed to get somewhere for some medical attention.

I gulped down what remained of the beer and set the mug on the bar. Truth be told, I didn't want to be anywhere near the boys right now. I just wanted to think. I reached into my pocket and dug out a couple of bucks, tossing them onto the counter next to the mug, and nodding at the bartender. "Thanks, Rhonda, I'm out of here."

"Jesus, Brake, ain't no need to go off in a lather." Red frowned at me, his brows drawing together.

"I ain't lathered; I just got things to do. I'll drop that load before I head for home."

Stepping past Billy, I approached Red as I walked toward the door.

"Maybe you ought to get yourself a tetanus shot," Billy said with a facetious tone apparent in his voice. It was obvious that Billy had already done some drinking, and I rolled my eyes. Without thinking, Red patted my back as I strolled past him and headed for the door. I flinched and grit my teeth as I sped up my pace heading out of the saloon.

Jogging across the parking lot, I climbed up into my rig and released the brakes. I was unable to ignore the pain of the birdshot lodged in my shoulder. I knew I couldn't see a doctor without a report being filed, so I drove a mile out of town and pulled up in front of Melissa Briggs's house. I figured with her being a rodeo gal, and having grown up with four brothers, she'd be none too squeamish about plucking a couple dozen pellets out of me.

Now I'll admit right here that Melissa and I have rolled around a bit and like each other plenty, but neither of us have a hankering for settling down and doing the family thing. She's quite easygoing, for a girl, and right sporting enough to be pals with.

Hopping down out of the truck, I strolled across the lawn and rapped on the front door of her brick, ranch-style house. A moment later I heard a noise inside, and Melissa opened the door. Just the sight of her temporarily erased the rest of the day from my mind. Blond and beautiful, her blue eyes gleamed brightly, and her full red lips formed a smile as she caught sight of me. She was barefooted, dressed in denim shorts, and wore no bra beneath her white t-shirt. Her physically fit body quickened my pulse which had an immediate and noticeable effect on my blood pressure elsewhere.

"Hey, Brady. How you doin', cowboy?"

"Hey, Mel." I leaned forward and kissed her hard on the lips.

"Well, you're mighty spry for a weeknight," she teased when we had stepped away from one another.

"Well, not exactly. I need you to tend to something for me if you have a minute."

"You ain't usually one for a quickie," she said with a giggle.

"You got that right." I smiled at her jest. "No, I've got me some scratches and a little birdshot in my upper arm and shoulder. Most of the pellets are just in the surface, but I need you to dig them out, if you don't mind."

"My God, Brady. What happened?"

Peeling away my shirt, I quickly made up a story in my head. I explained the 'accidental shooting in the presence of a 'friend' and then stood still as she looked me over.

"You probably ought to have a doctor look at these, Brady, but I'll take them out if that's what you want. I thought you said you just had some scratches; it looks like some big cat got a hold of you."

"Ah, nah, I fell down. Barbed wire or something I think."

"Yeah, okay, you don't have to explain it to me. Come on into bathroom where I have tweezers and peroxide, and we'll get you cleaned up."

"Thanks, Mel. As I said, it was an accident, and I don't want to get my friend into trouble with the authorities. You know how doctors are. They've got to fill out reports and all, and my buddy doesn't need this on his record. I really appreciate you doing this for me."

"Who was it that shot you if you don't mind my askin'?" she said as I followed her down the hall.

"I'd rather not say, Mel."

"Anything for you, Brady," she replied, patting me on the rump. "Now sit down here on the toilet, and we'll get this over with. Turn your back toward the light over the sink, so I can see what I'm doing."

Using tweezers, cotton swabs, and a little bit of hydrogen peroxide Mel removed the pellets dropping each one into a little cup she had placed next to the sink. The sound of the pellets striking the bottom of the cup confirmed my belief that it was steel shot. Once all of the shot had been removed she sanitized the wounds, including the gouges in my lower back, and covered everything with an antibiotic ointment, gauze, and adhesive tape. The minute the gauze and ointment went on I started to feel worlds better.

"There, that looks good to me," she said soothingly as she patted my shoulder lightly. Then, tugging on my shoulders, Mel pulled me around to face her. I found my face pressed firmly into the exposed flesh of her chest. She had pulled down the low-cut t-shirt and allowed it to ride up under her beautiful breasts. Ruffling my hair with her fingers, she smothered me playfully and began kissing me. Within minutes my pants were around my ankles, and she was planted firmly on my lap. I thanked her thoroughly before I left, and she was grateful I'd shown up to ask for the favor of her care.

Forty minutes after arriving at her door, and after promising a longer stay during my next visit, I left Melissa's house and hopped back into my rig. The pumping station was south of there by a few miles, and as I headed in that direction I marveled at how much better she'd made me feel.

Those few moments at Melissa's house had made me nearly forget about the incident at Ten Mile Fork, but as I sped along the roadway I wondered what had happened there. Those thoughts filled my mind as I watched the setting sun cast eerie shadows across the pavement and the miles and miles of fields around me. What kind of weird shit had I seen? The warmth of my visit with Mel faded, and I spent the rest of the drive to the pumping station and back watching for dust devils.

Two-and-a-half hours later, I pulled up in front of my house. It was located in the little town of Broken Spoke, Texas, a town settled in the mid 1800s where most of its residents descended from the original inhabitants. The downtown storefronts had long been vacated, the trains no longer stopped when they passed through twice a day, and tumbleweeds were known to blow down Main Street. Many residents had succumbed to the ease with which we can travel and the seduction of the flashy, lower-cost franchise businesses in the nearby cities and towns. Small, independent businesses couldn't compete, and the once-dazzling lights of our village center had slowly faded to gloom. Save for those working at the school, the cotton gin, and the franchise convenience store near the highway most of our residents worked in farming or for employers outside of town.

Setting the brakes and hitting the kill switch, I hopped down out of the rig. I had gone ten steps toward the house before I remembered the thing I'd ripped from the devil's neck. Walking back to the truck, I stepped around to the passenger side and opened the door to retrieve the necklace. Stuffing it into my pocket, I strode across the barren earth that served as my front lawn, leaped up onto the porch, and headed through the front door. The house I shared with my mother was a single story ranch with faded yellow vinyl siding that was still in good condition despite the sun's merciless baking.

"That you, Brady?" my mother called out from the kitchen as I entered the house. I glanced at the television where my mother's favorite crime drama played out its familiar plot. She spent most evenings seated in her wingback recliner watching a full slate of television dramas and sitcoms. And most nights I lovingly woke her and urged her to go to bed about the time the news anchors began to rattle off the headlines during the late newscast.

"Yeah, Momma, it's me."

"You feeling all right? You look a little pale," she said, looking up at me when I walked into the kitchen.

"Yeah, I'm fine." I sauntered over and kissed her lightly on a rose-colored cheek. A thin woman, her fifty years have been kind to her despite the endless hours she spent working at the local cotton gin. Her long, reddish hair, still pulled back in a ponytail, smelled of cottonseed. Dressed in denim pants and a white blouse, the woman moved effortlessly about the kitchen. Smoke curled towards the ceiling from the cigarette resting on an ashtray next to a half-empty bottle of beer on the small table.

Opening the refrigerator door I grabbed a beer, opened it, and took a long pull from the bottle. It tasted fantastic after the day I'd had, that was for sure. As I closed the door with my hip my mother turned and smiled at me.

"I'm making myself a snack. You want somethin'?"

"No, I'm fine. I'll be in my room for a while," I said as I stepped past her and made for the door.

"My Lord, Brady. Are you bleeding? What happened to your shirt? You look like you've been hit with a load of shot! You want me to call a doctor?"

"No. I'm fine, Momma. I fell into some barbed wire at one of the lease sites. Nothing to worry about," I replied as I continued down the hallway to my bedroom.

"That doesn't look like barbed wire to me. You in some kind of trouble?" Her voice followed me down the hall, and I glanced back to see her giving me the narrow-eyed look that said: *Brady, you're in trouble.*

"Momma, don't worry about it. I was out with some friends and moved when I shouldn't have. It ain't nothin'. Besides, I already had it looked at, and it's just fine."

I stepped into my room and closed the door behind me before she had time to argue my story. The fading sunset cast heavy shadows on the wall of the small, densely furnished room. Flicking on the light switch, I glanced about still feeling uneasy and out of sorts.

My bedroom was a hodgepodge of various things I'd collected over the course of my life. There were a few childhood toys and things that I didn't want to throw out: my trophies from the high-school football team, my baseball bat and glove for when the boys and I played Babe Ruth, and my collection of books and magazines. The walls were papered with posters for the Cowboys, and the floor carpeted in dirty clothes. The small, cramped space was kept cool by an air conditioning vent in the wall making the space livable compared to the raging heat outside.

Roger, Momma's last boyfriend, had installed central heating and air conditioning when he retired last summer. He'd been fifteen years older than she was and had retired with a pension from a large company over in Lubbock. Three months after his retirement party, he was killed driving home from a fishing trip. They'd all stopped off for a final round before splitting up to go home, and Roger had one too many. He'd crossed the centerline and collided with an on-coming tractor-trailer.

Damn shitty thing if you ask me. It ain't that he and I were close, as I never really cared for the man, but my mom adored him. They were set up to do a little traveling and spend some quality time together. Anyway, we buried him over across the railroad tracks in the old bone yard, and Momma went back to work at the gin.

Reaching into my pocket, I retrieved the amulet as I sat down on the edge of my unmade bed. The item felt odd in my hands as I turned it over and examined it. The braided cord was attached in two places to what actually appeared to be a pouch. The whole thing was decorated in an odd pattern of bone beads and porcupine quills. Now I'm no expert, but I decided immediately that it was something American Indian, and the leather looked old and cracked.

"It's not an amulet at all," I mused aloud, "but some kind of medicine bundle."

The tanned leather pouch was circular in shape and stitched tightly around the outer edges. Curiosity about the contents of this little bag filled me. Setting the empty beer bottle on the corner of my dresser, I pulled my pocketknife out of my jeans and began carefully cutting at the threads holding the bundle together. Before I could get very far a chilling surge of energy flowed through me and halted my investigation. The scowling face of the Indian flashed in my mind's eye, and a wave of fear swept through me. I hurled the pouch across the room where it landed atop some papers and slipped down through a pile of my belongings coming to rest somewhere near the desk. My heart pounded for a minute while I stared in the direction I'd tossed it. A sick feeling in my stomach overcame me, and I decided to let the damn thing stay where it had fallen for now.

I got to my feet and closed the knife slipping it back into my pocket. I sauntered down the short hallway and into the kitchen where I opened the refrigerator in search of another beer. I was disappointed to find only milk and soda in the icebox and was reminded of the fact that I had intended to grab some after work.

"Momma, I'm going over to Benny's for a beer," I called out, glancing into the living room where she sat watching the television. She rocked quietly in her chair, nibbling on tortilla chips and bean dip, completely immersed in the show. Hearing no response, I headed out the back door.

A few minutes later I approached the back door to Benny Rodriguez' house. Benny is known locally as a bootlegger. Living in a "dry" county (a county where the sale of alcohol is illegal) a bootlegger is really nothing more than a person who resells beer and liquor purchased in a nearby county where it's legal to buy alcohol. Benny was our party guy in high school. He always had booze and the best weed. He had continued that trend into adulthood and now served the members of our community with a convenience that was greatly appreciated. Inflated prices notwithstanding.

After downing a few brews at Benny's I returned to our backyard. In the twilight of the day's final hours I sat down on the bench of our wooden picnic table. Popping the cap off one of the six Lone Stars I had brought back I sat there for quite a while pondering what I had stumbled into today. As memories of the bizarre event toyed with my emotions I prayed silently that I may never see anything like it again.

Four beers later, and feeling pretty good, I decided to go in to bed. Just before turning out the light I remembered how my grade school teacher had me start a journal after my daddy abandoned us. I was pretty upset over that ordeal, and she thought it would help me get things off my mind. Seems it worked pretty well for me then. I rummaged through some old things from my high school days until I found a mostly empty notebook.

Not knowing where the heck this ordeal might lead, or if documenting what happened might disprove my insanity at some later date, I have begun this journal.

I pray this is the only entry.

❊ 3 ❊

Damn it," I muttered, hearing the ringtone of my cell phone from where it lay on the passenger's seat of the truck. I had just climbed the ladder on the crude oil storage tank to test the oil for my last lease of the day. I was hot, tired, and I just wanted to get this last load to the pump station and head to the saloon for a drink. "Well, they can leave a message, or it ain't that important." Since a cell phone had been attributed to starting a fire over in Houston it was regulation that we had to leave it inside the truck while performing our duties outside the cab.

I collected my samples and stowed them in the carrier before I closed the lid on the tank and climbed down the ladder. Slipping the tubes into the spinner, I checked for water and sediment and was writing my purchase ticket when the phone rang again. Annoyed, I leapt up into the cab and snatched it up off the seat.

"Yeah," I said, flipping the phone open and raising it to my cheek.

"Brake? It's Billy. You might want to stop what you're doing, and get home as quick as you can. Seems your momma had some trouble this afternoon. There were shots fired, and I guess somebody got killed at your house."

"What the hell?" I was stunned by the sudden news. "Billy, what happened?"

"I don't know no more than that, but you better haul ass over there. Where are you at anyway?"

"I'm at the Larkin/Caswell lease just north of Levelland. It's gonna take me forty minutes to get home. I just wrote a purchase ticket, but if it's all right with you I'll come back tomorrow and load her."

"That's fine, Brady. Just get home to your momma."

"Yup, plan to. I'm fixin' to call over there. Thanks, Billy," I replied, as my nerves splintered, and I was haunted by yesterday's events. Some part of me couldn't shake the idea that this was related to what I'd seen.

I hung up and immediately punched the speed dial to ring my house. Pulling the door closed, I hit the release buttons for the brakes and slipped my rig into gear. As the truck jerked and grunted its way clear of the tanks the phone stopped ringing and a man's voice answered.

"Drake residence."

"Who the hell is this?" I demanded none too amused that there was a strange man answering my home phone.

"This is Sheriff Hugh Baker." The man's voice was gravely, similar in tone to Billy Don's. "Who might *this* be?"

"This is Brady Drake, Sheriff, and that's my phone you're talking on. Where's my mother?"

"She's right here, Mr. Drake. Some paramedics are taking a look at her seeing as she got a little banged up this afternoon. I think she's gonna be all right. Look, I'd rather not discuss this over the phone, but I'd like to ask you a few questions. Where are you?"

"I'm on Route 385 north of Levelland, but I'll be on Route 114 shortly and expect to get there in about half an hour. I reckon it can wait until then?"

"Yes sir, that's fine. We'll still be here. I'll talk to you then."

Tapping the end button, I tucked the phone into the belt clip and focused on getting home. As I turned west at an intersection in the middle of Levelland, my phone rang again.

"Yeah?"

"Brady, I just got a call from Texas Highway Patrol and…"

Just then a grungy-looking punk with his ball cap on sideways swerved in and cut me off. He was so close I could see the gold chains around his neck and hear the pathetic excuse for music he was listening to on his half-blown stereo. Having to respond to the situation in order to avoid slamming my rig into his piece of crap car full on, I shouted into the phone.

"Yeah, Billy, I gotta go."

Dropping the phone into my lap, I cut the wheel while tapping my brakes and veering around a woman in a small sedan. With a lot of luck and a bit of skill I missed her, cleared the intersection, and followed the offending vehicle out of town.

"Asshole!" I hollered, experiencing a renewed sense of outrage as he sped away from me. I pulled the cord on my air horn a few times just to let him know how I felt about it. Pissed off and worried about my mom's well being, I stomped down on the accelerator getting every ounce of speed I could out of the rig.

While my anger at the kid faded I wondered if he was just another self-absorbed jerk speeding through town for the hell of it, or if maybe someone he cared about might also be in trouble. Maybe he, too, had seen something horrible and his seemingly senseless act was somehow justified. Despite my own prejudice I accepted the fact that maybe his problems were no less than mine. However, I wasn't endangering others. This reflection wouldn't mean squat to most people, but it suddenly meant a lot to me. And I usually ain't all that deep about things.

I fumbled around for my phone on the seat between my thighs. When I found it I snatched it up and slipped it back into the clip on my belt watching as the jackass in the hot rod disappeared down the highway in front of me.

Cars whizzed by me heading east as my truck rolled west on Route 114. Pump jacks, cotton fields, combines, and distant farmhouses filed by as I stared straight ahead desperate to reach my momma and our home.

It had been our home since my dad run off when I was about nine. He was a jack-of-all-trades and professional at none. My dad liked to drink beer, fight, and chase women. He had only worked when the spirit moved him, and that wasn't all that often. Seems no matter what he did my mom just ignored it and took care of us both.

My mom had always worked two jobs, and she tolerated him because "Well, he ain't been right since he came back from the war in Vietnam."

My Aunt Mary, my dad's sister, said "He weren't never right" and that my mom just made excuses for him because he was the only man she ever loved. Anyway, it's been Momma and me ever since the day he didn't come home from some roughneck job over near Odessa. He called me a couple of times the following year, and both times he was two sheets to the wind. He had babbled on about protecting me by being away or some shit. I don't pretend to know what he was talking about, but that's a whole other story. Besides, we ain't heard from him since.

I turned off the highway and drove into Broken Spoke, Texas population two hundred and eighty five. Even just getting onto East Street I could already see the lights of the ambulance and police units parked outside my house. Passing the convenience store and the large silos of the cotton gin my truck rattled and rolled down the street toward the little house I'd known my entire life as home which now looked like something out of a crime show segment on television.

Yellow tape ran from the handle of my parked pickup truck to the small desert willow tree on the other side of the yard, just in front of the house. The screen door, which appeared to have been ripped off the front of my house, lay in the yard off to one side of the small porch. The doorframe seemed slightly out of sorts, and one window to the left of the door was missing its glass pane. Only shards of its original whole remained. The local sheriff's car, a deputy's car, several Texas Highway Patrol cars, and two ambulances sat in various spots around the front of the house. One ambulance was pulling away as I pulled my truck off the road and parked in front of my neighbor's house. Hopping down from the cab, I hit the ground and ran toward my house.

"Hey, hey! Slow down there," a young Texas Highway Patrol officer barked as I approached the house.

"Where's my momma?" I demanded, heart in my throat.

"You need to stop, mister." His hands came up in front of him as a second officer came to his aid.

Stepping away from their outstretched hands I felt the anger rising as I clenched my fists at them. "Look, this is my house, and my mother is in there somewhere. Just get the hell out of my way!"

"Let him through," bellowed a large man dressed in the uniform of a County Sheriff. He stepped down from the front porch and walked in my direction. He was a tall man with thick-rimmed glasses parked on the nose beneath his Stetson. The guy looked like a preacher who might have lost his way with the Lord and went into law enforcement.

"Go ahead," said the second highway patrolman as I pushed by ignoring his light grasp of my arm and shoulder. I sprinted across the sun-baked remnants of my front lawn.

"Easy now, young man. You must be Brady Drake. Claudia Drake is your mother?"

"Yes, I'm Brady Drake, sir. I need to see my mother."

"Mr. Drake, I'm Sheriff Baker, we talked briefly on the phone." The big man didn't seem inclined to let me go just yet.

"Yeah, Sheriff. Where's my mother!" I sputtered in a tone bordering on hysteria.

"Mr. Drake, your mother is being looked after, and you need to slow things down here so as we can have us a talk."

"Brady!" My mom called out from off to my right.

Turning, I was relieved to see her sitting calmly just inside the back door of the remaining ambulance which was parked close to the house. A paramedic was working on her applying gauze and bandages to a bloody crease on the left side of her scalp. Her wrist was splinted, and I was shocked to see her blouse open, her bra-covered breast exposed, and white tape around her midriff.

Running to her and ignoring the Sheriff's orders that I "get back there this instant" I carefully hugged her as she began to sob.

"My Lord, Brady, it was terrifying! I've never been so scared in my life. He came out of nowhere. He had big, scary eyes, and he looked awful, and…"

"Easy, Momma, easy," I said, patting her gently on the arm and kissing her lightly on the forehead while I made sure to stay clear of the paramedic's hands as she worked. Momma's reference to the "big, scary eyes" caused a knot to form in my stomach.

"She's fixin' to be fine," the woman assured me as the scissors in her left hand snipped the final piece of tape. "We're going to take her in for some tests, but she doesn't seem to have any life-threatening injuries. Some of her ribs are cracked, her wrist is severely sprained, possibly broken, and this head wound is likely to have caused a mild concussion. We'll be taking her to Covenant Hospital in Levelland. Things should check out just fine, though, and they'll probably release her after that. You're welcome to follow along and retrieve her once we're through."

"Thank you, ma'am," I responded.

Tossing the implements of her trade back into her kit, the woman turned away as a second paramedic approached to help her pack up. I was grateful to have a moment to console my mother.

"He was horrifying, Brady. That man just burst into the house; he tore the door right off. I ain't never seen a man as scary looking as he was, Brady. I swear I never have. My God, he looked like the devil himself. And poor Donny Jones…" A muffled shriek left her lips with the memory. "Poor Donny! He *killed* Donny, Brady. He was so strong. He took Donny's gun away from him then twisted him like this," she said, miming the movement in the air with tears running down her face, "and snapped his neck like he was nothin' more than a rag doll." She then started to sob as the paramedic came up alongside us.

"I'll take her from here, Mr. Drake. She's fixin' to be right fine. You come along and fetch her later on, alright?"

"Give me another minute, will you?" My mother looked up at the paramedic hopefully.

"Brady, we need to talk with you." We were interrupted by the local constable, a stocky man with red hair, mustache, and twinkling blue eyes. He was shadowed by the impatient shadow of the sheriff who was skulking behind him.

Being a small town we have Constable Edward Wharem who handles minor things like traffic tickets and so on. He has always worked a regular job and is available mostly on nights and weekends.

Any serious problems are handled by the police from Levelland which was only ten miles away or by the county sheriff department. In a case like this both departments felt compelled to get involved along with the Highway Patrol. Then again, this was a murder, and those weren't real common in our neck of the woods.

Constable Wharem and I had grown up together. We'd dated some of the same girls, played sports on the same teams, and even managed to get hauled in together when we were in junior high school for toilet papering the tree on the principal's front lawn.

"Yeah, Eddie. Okay."

"Let's get you to the hospital, Mrs. Drake." The paramedic gently guided her deeper into the vehicle.

"Brady, you ain't in no trouble, are ya?" my mother asked, reaching out to me with her good hand.

"No Momma, I ain't in trouble." I grasped her hand and squeezed it gently. I looked her in the eye, attempting to reassure her that everything was gonna be okay, before letting her go. "You go along with them. I'll be along to fetch you once I've talked with the Sheriff. I promise I'll be along shortly."

She seemed resolved to go along to the hospital, and I turned away as the second paramedic closed the doors.

"Damn strange thing," Eddie said as we walked together toward Sheriff Baker and his ring of deputies. "You any idea who might have done this, Brady?"

"No, no idea. It's awfully weird; I honestly can't believe it." In the back of my mind I had a feeling that it more than likely related to the strange shit I had seen yesterday.

As we approached the sheriff the ambulance pulled out of the yard, with its lights shimmering. "Mr. Drake, we ain't accustomed to having violent crimes like this in Broken Spoke. And only a damn few of them in this county, for that matter. You got any idea why someone would break into your house, accost your mother, and kill the neighbor when he came to her aid?" Sheriff Baker was obviously annoyed by my response to him earlier. I struggled to find the words to reply as I got within a few feet of him.

The Indian immediately came to mind, but I found it hard to make it all fit together. The pouch I'd taken from him seemed like the probable reason, but I wasn't positively sure it was him who had done all this. If it was him… Well, I was feeling real damn reluctant to try and explain something that I neither understood nor quite believed. So I did the one thing I've always done when unsure of where the situation might be headed: I denied any knowledge of anything.

"No, I can't think of any reason or any*one* for that matter. What happened anyway?"

"You ain't tied up in liquor, drugs, illegal immigrants, or anything like that, are you Mr. Drake?"

I didn't care for the Sheriff's accusations, but at the same time I tried *real* hard not to take offense to it. I knew he was just trying to figure things out, but if that Indian was the guy who killed Donny the Sheriff wouldn't believe any attempt I might make to explain it.

"Hell no!" I said, truly annoyed while hoping to put on a convincing performance. Even though I was answering truthfully deep down I was feeling guilty knowing what I knew. "Look, we're the victims here. I have no idea who did this, but I would appreciate it if you would tell me what the hell happened here. And what the fuck happened to poor Donny Jones?"

"Well, you can help things a whole lot if you would mind your language. As a lawman and as a Christian I'm not accustomed to having innocent folk cursing at me. Guilty bastards yes, but not good, God fearing folk. You think you can control that, Mr. Drake?" Sheriff Baker's face betrayed his disdain.

"Yes sir, my apology," I sputtered, hoping to avoid any further suspicion. Hell, I hadn't done a freakin' thing, but I was still feeling guilty. And that alone is a damn sure way to end up going to jail.

"Fine then. According to the report your mother gave me some half-naked young heathen sporting long, black hair and strange black eyes ripped the screen door off the hinges, kicked in the front door and entered the house. She said it seemed like he was looking for something. When Claudia approached him he attacked her and likely would have killed her if Donny Jones hadn't seen the bastard enter the house and come a runnin'."

"Well, you know Donny," Constable Wharem interjected. "Always packing his .38 revolver. He went in and pulled the gun out of his boot before he ordered the intruder to step away from your mother. Then the bastard grabbed her by the wrist and flung her across the room at Donny. She slammed into him and knocked him down. Claudia guessed it weren't ten seconds before the intruder had taken Donny's gun, snapped his neck, and flung him across the room."

"Seems Donny had called 911 on his cell phone," Sheriff Baker interrupted, shooting Constable Wharem a glare, "while he was running toward the house. My deputy there, Bobby Dawson, was patrolling south of town when he got the call from dispatch. He says the man skedaddled, and he caught just a glimpse of him before he disappeared in the cotton field over yonder. They've put out an APB for a man about six feet tall, long black hair, Mexican maybe, and wearing denim pants and no shirt. The son-of-a-bitch has Donny's gun."

"You know anybody that matches that description?" Sheriff Baker asked as his eyes probed mine to see if there was anything else I could be hiding.

"No Sheriff," I said, letting it roll smoothly off my tongue, "can't say that I do." The way I said it, it didn't feel like a lie to me.

Another patrol car arrived in front of the house, and we all turned to watch as a Texas Highway Patrol officer sauntered up to us with another trooper right on his heels. He looked at the others before turning his attention to me. "You Brady Drake?" the man asked.

"Yes, sir."

"Mr. Drake, I'm Sergeant Dickens, Texas Highway Patrol. Kind of a coincidence arriving here to find your place is a crime scene seeing as I've some questions about a situation happened yesterday down near Plains at a little spot called Ten Mile Fork. You were down that'a way yesterday, weren't you?"

Sweat broke out on my scalp, and I felt as though the world was crawling up my ass. There wasn't a damn thing I could do at that moment but to answer the man as best I could. "Yeah, I went through there. What's this all about?"

"Did you stop at the old Texaco station there? And, if not, did you see anything unusual while you was passing through?"

I felt guilt welling up, seeping out from under my skin, and I feared the flush sensation I was feeling in my neck and face was going to give me away. Despite the fact that I'd done nothing wrong I lied anyway.

"Ah, nah, nope, I don't remember seeing anything."

Sergeant Dickens stared at me, and, despite the shadows caused by his sunglasses, I sensed doubt in his glowering eyes.

He knows I'm lying.

"Odd thing Mr. Drake. Seeing as a combine driver spotted your rig flying up the highway away from Ten Mile Fork just seconds after an explosion that about rocked the whole damn county. He said it was a bright orange cab with the blue Smith Oil Transport logo on the side. I called the company and talked to your boss, and he said you were the only driver in that area yesterday. So how is it that the entire gas station, farm house, and fuel pumps were blown sky high and you didn't see or hear anything unusual?"

Must have been why Billy called me that second time! I thought, remembering now that he had mentioned the Texas Highway Patrol before I dropped my phone.

Panic crept up my spine. Vivid memories of the wind driven mini-twister, and what happened after flooded my mind's eye. Right about then a part of me wanted to tell the whole truth.

The moment passed and I realized no one would believe me. I just couldn't tell them about what really happened out there at Ten Mile Fork. Had I not seen it myself I wouldn't believe it either.

So how the hell was I going to convince the Texas Highway Patrol that I saw what I saw and not look like a damn idiot telling lies? Or, worse, like a killer covering his tracks. Add onto that trying to convince them that now some demon was here breaking into my house, beating up my momma, and killing one of my neighbors. Hell, just thinking about it, I felt as though I was only two lug nuts shy of the wheels coming off, and the whole damn mess would send me careening down the highway to the nut house or prison.

"Hell, I don't know. I had the radio turned up pretty loud. Maybe I just thought it was part of the music. I don't know!" I muttered defensively.

All six of the lawmen looked at me with an expression that said they thought I was plum full of bullshit, and they didn't like my tone of voice. I suppose the way I was twisting and looking off didn't help my case any. But, that was my story, and they must have realized that I was sticking to it.

Rocking for a moment on the balls of his feet with his cowboy boots grinding into the dust where my lawn ought to be Sergeant Dickens fiddled with his hat for a moment and spoke again. "And, just so I can clarify this in my mind, you're *sure* you didn't stop there at the gas station?"

"No. I told you I don't know anything about the place. I just passed through there on my way to the pumping station."

"Uh-huh." The sergeant turned his head and looked at Sheriff Baker. "Hugh, I'm going to leave him to you, but don't let him go too far. It's more than likely we'll be coming back to have another chat with him *real* soon."

Turning back to me, Sergeant Dickens lowered his voice and drew his sunglasses down, so I could see the look of distrust in his piercing gaze. "Mr. Drake, I think you're hiding something, but until I find out what it is I'm going to have to let you go on about your business. You make sure you stick around, you hear?"

Not wanting to antagonize the officer further I simply nodded my head.

Pushing his sunglasses back up his nose until they covered his eyes, he turned, and together the two highway patrolmen stalked off toward their cruiser. Sheriff Baker stepped closer to me.

"Young man, if I was you, I'd want to get this out in the open. Seems whoever it is that came in here weren't screwin' around if you catch my meaning. Seeing as he got run off it ain't likely he got whatever it was he came after, so it's real likely he's fixin' to come on back.

Your momma might not be quite so lucky next time, and I don't believe you'd fare much better if he's as nasty as he sounds. That said, is there anything else you can tell me?"

The thought of running into that dust devil again was less than appealing to me, but I didn't believe for a minute that trying to explain things to this cop was going to be of any help. Especially now, after I had denied knowing anything about it.

"I told you I don't know anything!" I snapped.

His eyes narrowed, and he stepped backward. "Okay, fine, it's your funeral, boy. But if you decide to fess-up you go on and give me a call. Eddie, you keep an eye on this place, and my men will do the same."

"You bet, Hugh," Constable Wharem responded.

With that the Sheriff turned and strode away.

Eddie watched the sheriff and deputies as they returned to their cruisers. Then he looked me in the eye and gripped me firmly by my good shoulder. "Brady, you take it easy. I've got to go. I'll keep an eye on your place, and if this bastard returns we'll nail him. You need anything, or you feel as though you need to talk, you call me. I'm sure that we all will get through this whatever it is that's going on."

Knowing he had his own doubts and was reaching out to me anyway I was doubly grateful for his friendship. "Thanks, Eddie."

He nodded before he strode across the lawn and climbed into his Ford pickup truck.

Relieved to have the questioning behind me, I tried to go into the house, but the officer at the door wouldn't allow me in until they had dusted for prints and finished investigating. Reluctantly, I left the front porch and sauntered over to lean against the side of my pickup truck, where I stood waiting sheltered from the late day sun by the shade of a cottonwood tree.

I stood there for about an hour, watching, waiting, and fearful one of the officers would leave the house with that tiny sack.

Why was I worried? Damned if I know, but I felt drawn to it now for some reason. I guess part of me also hoped that the creature had found it and was now gone from my life. Either way, I didn't want to see that Indian artifact leave the house in the hands of one of the officers because it was also likely to initiate another round of questions. Then again, I was probably overreacting. They didn't have a clue what I saw yesterday. It was more than likely that they would pay it no mind since similar, although less authentic, items are available at powwows and tourist shops over in New Mexico.

It occurred to me as I was standing there that I had thought of this guy as a dust devil, and I began to wonder if that was the reason those tiny dirt twisters were referred to as such. Seemed reasonable to me that anyone who had seen what I had would make just such a correlation between the two. Interesting bit of information to consider I guess, but if that was the case why hadn't anyone ever mentioned it? Huh, funny I should ask that question.

After another forty minutes of coming and going the police investigation unit finally packed up their gear and left me standing alone in my yard.

Relieved to finally have my home empty of people, I headed inside. What I saw stopped me, and I could feel a complicated mix of sorrow and rage pooling in the pit of my stomach. The entire front room had been ransacked, and the furnishings completely destroyed. Lamps were broken, end tables and chairs overturned, and the cherry coffee table lay split in half and upturned on the carpet. The television, its thirty-two inch screen shattered, lay sideways on the floor. Blood stained the center of the plush, beige carpet, and a bullet hole was clearly visible in the center of the wall at the back of the room. I headed into the small hallway at center of the house and looked into the kitchen where the table had been overturned and food and dishes scattered about the floor.

Turning back to look at the massive blood stain, I thought of Donny Jones. Donny was a small, tenacious man who worked hard and had raised a family of five. He was a man I had known all my life. I never would have suspected he would die in the middle of my living room trying to protect my mother.

Things have taken a real strange turn since I stopped for that damn Yoohoo.

I stepped past the bathroom and pushed open the door to my bedroom. Nothing inside had been disturbed; it was as I had left it: in its usual organized disarray. I strode across the room and began digging through the mess around my desk. After a couple moments of rooting around I spotted the pouch pinched between the side of my desk and a stack of girly magazines.

I reached out, grabbed the medicine bundle, and managed to finger the lanyard from the angle I had. Not wanting to dislodge the magazines or move my desk, I decided to carefully work the little medicine bundle free. It came loose after a moment or so, and as I squirmed out from beneath the desk the lanyard wrapped around my fingers and the pouch dangled beneath them. At the contact with the thing I felt an eerie chill overtaking me. It caused a tingling sensation in my fingers, and I felt a presence, then a sort of connection. At least that's the best way to describe it. Standing there with the medicine bundle swaying below my hand I wondered what the hell I was going to do with it.

My first thought was to take it out back where I could start a fire in the burn barrel and destroy it. But then I considered that I might need it for proof later on? And what might happen if I *did* burn it? I stood there, numb with indecision, for a long while. Each idea that surfaced was dismissed just as quickly as the last had been and none of them would work.

Then the thought occurred to me that he must have some kind of connection to the damn medicine bundle like it had some kind of homing device or something, because how else would he have known where to look for it? He couldn't have a clue as to my identity, so it ain't as though he could have looked me up in the phone book.

I finally decided to just wrap it in something and keep it with me in the truck until I figured out what to do with it. At least that way my momma wouldn't be exposed to him again.

Remembering a blue velvet bag I had kept from a bottle of Crown Royal whiskey a friend had given me, I rifled through my desk drawers until I found it. I dumped out the Sacagawea dollar coins I was storing in there and placed the pouch inside. Pulling the drawstring tight, I made my way through the house. I stepped outside and pulled the broken door closed behind me causing the damaged hinges to give out a protesting screech. My eyes scanned the area nervously as I jogged across the yard and tugged open the passenger side door of my truck. I shoved the blue-wrapped pouch into the tool satchel I kept behind the seat and then climbed back out of the truck.

I felt a certain amount of relief after getting the thing out of the house. Leaping to the ground, I locked the rig and returned to my pickup. Thirty minutes later, I stood in the emergency room of Covenant Memorial Hospital in Levelland, waiting patiently next to my mother while the administrative staff discharged her.

The rest of the night was fairly quiet, and Momma was home. I couldn't say for sure that she was *safe*, but at least she was home. As for me, I felt as if I was going mad. Stark raving, Loony Tunes mad. Every second that ticked by felt as though it was an hour. Every creak of the old house, every noise outside or whisper of the wind set my nerves on edge. I didn't know what was coming next, but, deep down in my guts, I feared it wasn't going to be good. I wished I knew what to do about it, but… shit, I think I hear something.

✳ 4 ✳

But they know you was at that goddamn gas station, Brady! They matched the tire tread marks in the dirt to the tires on our rigs. They know all my trucks have the same tires because I told them they do. And it weren't like I could lie to 'em. Jesus, Brady, what the hell is going on with you, anyhow?"

Beneath his freshly brushed cowboy hat and sunglasses Billy Don's face was beet red. I tried not to look at him, hating my reflection in his mirrored lenses. It was the reflection of a man who knew he was in deep shit and didn't have the balls to tell anyone. J.J. and Red looked on with a mix of wariness and amusement.

"Hell, they told me a man was found dead, burned to near unrecognizable," Billy Don continued, "and his daughter ain't been seen since. All they found was a piece of the woman's shirt all torn up and ragged like. It don't look too damn good if you know what I mean. Whatever the hell happened down there you need to speak up. You got me worried here, Brady. I mean I know you're a good man and all that, but if something happened, some freak accident, or you freaked out, or whatever, you need to 'fess up."

"You think *I* killed those people, Billy? For Christ's sake I thought you knew me better than that," I replied with a deep frown. It was downright hurtful that my closest friends thought I could do something like that.

"Now, Brady, I ain't saying that. I just don't know what to believe. I don't believe you killed those folks or set that goddamned fire, but you must have seen something. You've got to know *something* about what went on down there. I mean, if you think about it, Brakesy, you've got to admit things are looking a tad bit suspicious."

I could feel Billy Don's piercing eyes glaring at me from behind the lenses of his wire-rimmed sunglasses. The intensity of his anger, mixed with the slur of his drawl, cut me like a razor. Despite the fact that it was well before noon I could tell he'd been drinking already. When he was stressed he hit the booze early.

I felt for the man. He was a good friend and a man who had always treated me like his own son. And I have to say I understood his point of view, but I didn't care for the accusatory tone in his voice. The anger welling up inside me was tempered only by the fact that I knew he was right about me knowing something. Deep down I agreed and thought some explanation was owed them. Despite that, I couldn't make myself say a damn thing about what happened. How could I? I was even starting to doubt my own sanity by that point.

Besides, my head was splitting with the remnants of a hangover from a late night of drinking over at the bootlegger's house. I had wandered over there after investigating the noises I heard while finishing up last night's journal entry.

"Come on, Brake, you can tell us. We're your friends, and we ain't going to rat you out." J.J. said quietly from where he stood leaning against the fender of my rig. He hadn't said a word to me at breakfast, and that's unusual for him. We've been close friends since grade school—we've been on fishing and hunting trips together, and he still lives just a few houses down from me. Since I hadn't said a word to him about this whole mess I guess he sensed something was amiss. At the very least, I'm sure he'd been wondering why I hadn't given him the low down.

Fact is, breakfast had been a quick and quiet affair. I had drunk more than my share of beer and whiskey last night at Benny's place, and my search around the outside of the house had proved to be nothing more than a trash can turning over in the wind. The music coming from the back of the bootlegger's house had drawn me across the backyards of my neighbors and into the well-lit and illegal establishment. Inside, a dozen people I knew sat watching a ballgame on television and drowning their own sorrows and regrets in the solace of what Benny had to offer.

I must've sat there half the night in that back room, my head ripe with images of what had gone on at Ten Mile Fork, and burning with guilt over the death of Donny Jones and what had happened to my mother. I, too, sought solace in liquor and hoped to hide from the world by descending into the shadows of an alcohol-induced fog. It didn't work, but the pain I suffered in the morning from the hangover forced me to focus on the immediate for a little bit. I guess you could say it sort of worked in that regard.

As if being drunk weren't enough, I'd woken up after that damned nightmare. It was a nightmare I had several times as a kid but only once or twice as an adult. In the dream I was some sort of cavalry soldier on horseback charging into a village of American Indians. My cutlass ruthlessly hacked a swath through a sea of frightened people. Blood was everywhere, and I was fueled by a desire to kill all before me. Suddenly, I was face to face with two small children, their eyes glaring up at me in terror. Then everything went black, then white, and I woke up. It was always the same and left me shaken with an incredible empty feeling. No sooner had I drifted back to sleep when the face of that damned dust devil began to haunt me and I was jerked awake again. Dreams are damn strange things if you ask me. That being said, I was feeling like shit this morning and didn't have the stomach to eat very much. I had still forced down some toast and a cup of coffee.

All I could think about now was the police wanting to pin that fire and those deaths on me and about my momma sitting at home recovering from her incident with that damn demon. "Demon" is the best thing I can think of at the moment to call the bastard because I don't have a clue what the hell he is. Again, it occurred to me that some people call whirlwinds "dust devils." I guess now I know why, although I don't remember anyone ever mentioning anything like this before. It seems to me if anyone had seen anything like this before we'd all know about it. But then I can't seem to tell anyone, so how's that for logic?

All I know is that since Ten Mile Fork fear had been my constant companion, and for the last two nights I just wanted to be around people. It didn't matter who it was as long as they were there and as long as they didn't want to talk to me.

"I don't want to talk about it," I said, backing away from them and stepping closer to the door of the truck.

Having never been good with being real close to people or keeping up a long-term romantic relationship my work has been the center of my world. And whenever anything goes awry in my life working is always the one thing that makes me feel normal again.

Billy Don stepped in my direction. Not a man who minces words you always knew where he stood, and if you didn't he was always willing to clarify his position. "I hate to say this, Brady, but I ain't so sure you ought to be out running about in that truck if things ain't right with you. This is dangerous work, and if you ain't right in the head… You can see what I mean."

That pissed me off. I'd worked for this man since I graduated from high school, and here he was questioning whether or not I was capable of doing my job. "What are you saying, Billy? You gonna take my truck away?"

"Well now, I ain't saying that, but I can't have you runnin' about if your head ain't screwed on right."

"So what the hell *are* you tellin' me?"

"I ain't tellin' you a goddamned thing. Don't be raisin' your fuckin' voice to me. I just want you to be damned sure you ain't gonna get involved with any more bullshit that might reflect poorly on yourself or this outfit."

"Why you fuckin' with me, Billy? You believe the cops over me?"

"Brady, I'm your damned friend. I ain't fuckin' with you. I just want to be sure you ain't gonna hurt yourself or end up in prison. If you don't understand that then maybe we ain't the friends I think we are."

"Easy, boys," Red said trying to break the growing tension.

I could have easily vented my rage and frustration on Billy Don. Instead I told myself to relax as I realized he was concerned about my welfare. If things were turned around I'd be just as concerned about him as he was about me and probably a bit suspicious.

"Look Billy, I ain't done nothing wrong. You got my word on that. So just let me go to work. I know I got a little explaining to do, but I need a little more time to set things straight in my head."

Looking each man in the eye, Billy Don, J.J., and Red, I realized I could trust them, and even if they didn't believe me I felt I really needed to tell *somebody*. "Look, let's just get today's work done," I said, "and I'll tell you boys what I can when we meet up tonight. That seem fair to ya'll?"

The three of them looked at one another then back at me. They nodded their heads and murmured consent to my proposal.

"Great. We'll hook up at the Cactus Creek after work, and I'll spill my guts."

With that we dispersed, each of us mounting our individual rigs and heading out across the arid lands of northwest Texas to service the lease assignments given out this morning. I was heading south, toward Sundown, and glad to have the roadway passing quickly beneath my wheels. I pulled the cell phone from the clip on my belt and dialed my home phone.

"Hello?"

"Hi, Momma. How're you doing this morning?"

"I'm fine, Brady. A little sore, but I'm okay. I called Caroline this morning and told her how sorry I am about Donny. I told her how brave he was and that I'd be dead if he hadn't come to my rescue. She just went all to tears on me, and it made me feel absolutely terrible." A muffled sob slipped through the phone. It choked me up that she was hurting so bad. "You know they've been together since junior high school. That's a rarity these days. Poor Caroline. She's gonna be lost without him."

"I know, Momma. Donny was a good egg."

A moment of silence passed between us.

"I've got a chicken stew on; I'm gonna take it over to her later today. Poor thing. She ain't going to feel much like cooking or eating. But chicken stew is a comforting thing…" Her voice trailed off.

The silence was awkward, but I wasn't sure what to say to her. All I wanted was for her to be all right. "How you holding up otherwise, Momma? How're you feeling?"

"I'm okay, Brady. Ribs hurt something awful if I breathe too deep, and I ain't used to having a busted wrist, so I keep trying to use it. It's painful, but I'll manage. Don't you worry about me. You just do what you've got to do. I suspect that man was just some drug fiend looking for some spare cash. He's likely far, far away by now."

Her tone of voice told me that she didn't believe it was over. I recognized that she was trying to put yesterday behind her. But, in some way, maybe it was some sort of intuition on both our parts, I guess. And, at that moment, I felt unable to assure her otherwise.

When silence filled the space between us I realized she wasn't much for conversation, so I decided to let her go for the time being. "You call me today if you need anything. You hear me?"

When there was no reply I thought I'd lost the phone connection. "Momma, are you there?"

"Yes, I'm here. But, Brady—" She paused. "I'm scared."

Her words hit me hard, and my heart ached. I ain't ever heard my Momma say she was scared. I heard her sniff a couple times, and the tear that crept into the corner of my eye startled me. It had been years since anyone had brought a tear to my eye and a long time since my heart had felt an ache like this. Realizing I was indirectly responsible for her pain I felt unable to console her. The only comfort I had to offer her at the moment was a lie.

"I know. I'm sorry. I'm sure you'll be safe. Maybe you ought not sit home alone if you feel uncomfortable. Why don't you go over to Aunt Mary or Aunt Karen's house, or go spend the day at your friend, Sofia's, house. You know you like to visit Sofia, and she always has something cooking in the kitchen." I thought of Sofia briefly: a good Catholic woman with statues of the Virgin Mary and crucifixes decorating her house. Seemed to me Momma would be as safe there as anywhere.

Silence was the only response I got.

"Momma?"

"Yes, Brady, yes. I might do something. Now you go ahead and get your work done; don't you worry about me. I'll be fine. This soup will be done soon, and I'll take it over to Caroline's. I'll see you tonight when you get home."

"Okay, Momma. I'll see you tonight. Remember: call me if you need anything."

"I will, Brady, you have a good day. I love you."

The phone clicked, the connection went dead, and the aura of her fear and sadness hung in the silence. Returning the phone to my belt clip, I focused on the road ahead and prayed that things would just return to normal.

Five minutes later I pulled off the roadway—still battling the guilt and ghastly images haunting my mind. Steering the rig between two houses, I guided it down a long dirt driveway to the lease tanks in the back yard of the larger of the two dwellings. I pulled the truck up alongside a large horse-head pump jack and three storage tanks and slipped the gearshift into neutral. I pulled my cell phone out of the clip on my belt and laid it on the console.

As I stepped down out of the truck the barking of a dog drew my attention toward the house, and I watched as an Irish setter bounded across the sun-baked lawn in my direction.

"Hey, Rufus!" I reached down with my gloved left hand and ruffled the dog's furry head and ears. His tail wagging, Rufus yelped nuzzling me in a playful way.

The back door of the house swung open, and a small, swarthy man with jet-black hair peered out at me. Dressed in denim pants and a white dress shirt he had a welcoming smile on his face.

"Hey, Brady, how are you this beautiful morning?" Hector Morales sang out, his English tinged with a hint of a Spanish accent.

"Fine, Hector. And you?"

"Wonderful. Elsa is fixing some *juevos con chilies*, *frijoles fritos*, and a stack of *tortillas*. Why don't you come in for breakfast when you're finished there? I've some fresh orange juice from my cousin in the Valley. Come in and join us, and we can chat while we eat."

I must admit I was beginning to feel a bit hungry. The affects of the hangover were waning, and my meager breakfast hadn't given me quite enough fuel for the day. Having eaten with the Morales family on several other occasions the thought of freshly prepared *tortillas*, eggs, and beans really set my hunger pangs in motion.

"That sounds way too good to turn down. I'll be in as soon as I get loaded."

"*Muy bien,*" Hector replied, and stepped back inside.

Still tussling playfully with Rufus I turned away from the animal, gathered up my kit and jogged across the barren ground. On reaching the ladder, I climbed onto the small platform atop the largest tank.

I hadn't really noticed the breeze blowing across the open prairie until I reached the top of the ladder. It was refreshing and carried remnants of the cooler, early-morning air. The familiar scents of earth and crude oil filled the gentle wind. Looking out across the great expanse of open land the drifting sand of an unplanted field gave me pause, my memory filling with the memories of the girl at Ten Mile Fork. I shook the image from my mind and returned to the task at hand. A few minutes later, with samples tucked snugly back into my tool kit, I grasped the handle of the metal box and started down the ladder.

A 'shift in energy' is the only way I can explain what I felt in that moment. It was like a sinking feeling in the pit of my stomach or kind of a cold sensation. It's like being alone on a dark night or passing by a cemetery: that eerie sensation that you can't quite put a finger on. A shiver shot up my spine, and the hair bristled on the back of my neck when I heard the driver-side door creak open on my truck. Spinning to look, my head pounding from the liquor I had consumed the night before, I could have pissed my pants when I spotted the demon from Ten Mile Fork climbing into the cab.

Señor Morales must have seen the bastard from inside the house because the next thing I knew Hector was coming around the corner of the building and heading toward my truck. Even more shocking was that he sported a double-barreled shotgun.

Hector was a decent man. He'd made his money operating a bricklaying company now run by his two sons. With his share of the company profits, along with his stipend from the oil lease on his property, he managed to have a good deal of leisure time. Semi-retired at age fifty, Hector was laid back and liked being home. It was here that friends and family spent a lot of time with him and his wife, Elsa. His eldest boy, Carlos, and his wife, Maria, lived next door. Raising his bushy, black eyebrows he glanced at me as he approached the rig.

"You know this *pendejo*, Brady?" he asked, wariness evident in his voice. "Cause he's fixin' to get a taste of rock salt in his ass if you don't."

Still stunned by the demon's appearance, I struggled to answer. "Ah, no. No, Hector, I don't know him."

Leaping down from the ladder, I ran to the passenger side of the rig and hopped up onto the step. I whipped the door open and stared directly into the enlarged black eyes of the longhaired demon.

"Get the *hell* out of my truck," I screamed with fear laced contempt. The creature simply glared at me while his liver colored lips formed a smirk, causing a creased scar on his upper lip to pucker. It was in that instant that I named the bastard Scar Lip.

Scar Lip dove across the cab, tackling me and driving both of us out away from the truck. Falling with the devil atop me, the impact was powerful, and I lost my breath when we hit the ground. The demon, already squatting over me, brought his fist down with incredible speed smashing me hard in the nose. I was lost in shock and fear and struggled for a moment before instinctively swinging my right arm upward with all the strength I could muster. The tool kit, still clenched tightly in hand, collided with the side of Scar Lip's head. Test tubes, rags, the dipping unit, and the other odds and ends I had in the box rained down on me as the man flipped sideways and rolled into the dirt beside me. I scrambled to my feet and ran around the truck, reached behind my seat, and grabbed the steel bar I used to thump my tires when checking for flats.

Hector, moving around so as to draw a bead on the attacker, raised his face from the weapon. "Hey, where'd he go?"

I slithered across the ground under the tanker and heard Scar Lip stumbling up behind me. I spun instinctively and whipped the bar around, catching him in the jaw just as he lurched at me. The contact was enough to stifle the howl he had opened his mouth to emit. Hector darted back across the yard as the attacker fell semi-conscious to the ground. He lowered his weapon as the being writhed in shock and agony on the dusty earth.

"I'll call the police," Hector growled, moving across the driveway toward the back door of the house. I turned to acknowledge him, but my lips moved and nothing came out. In that moment a twisting gale of sand was already wrapping around him.

Noise erupted from my throat, but the words were barely audible over the roar of the whirlwind. A horrendous gurgling and snapping sound erupted from the sand mass as it engulfed a startled Hector. The sounds reminded me of someone disassembling a raw chicken by brute force. The shotgun flew from his hands landing a good twelve feet in front of the truck. Fear forced its way through my veins, but I forced my feet to move as I dove toward the weapon, dodging a belt buckle as it whizzed past my head.

Just as the whirlwind began to subside, a second devil stepped from the tempest. Elsa, Hector's wife, appeared in the open doorway shielded from the world only by the thin screen stretched across the framework of the wooden door.

"Hector?" she called her voice wavering with nervous tension.

"Elsa, get back inside," I shouted, but it was already too late.

The demon that had emerged from Hector's body was larger than the first and sported a Mohawk (which immediately became his designation), and he was storming towards her.

She stood, eyes wide, frozen by fear, and I watched as the demon's hand burst through the screen mesh and grabbed her head. The noise was sickening as the bones broke in her face. Elsa's cry was cut short as the demon tightened its grip and yanked her through the door severing her spinal cord. A moment later Mohawk flung her twitching body through the air. Her corpse slammed into the side of the tanker-trailer. Blood spattered about the oval shaped steel before she fell to the barren ground sending a cloud of dust wafting upward.

I trained the gun on this new fiend aiming at a pouch hanging from around his neck as he lurched toward me. Rufus charged through the open doorway and past the ragged remnants of the screen door bearing down on Scar Lip.

The lack of recoil surprised me as I fired the shotgun. The first round of twelve-gauge rock salt spattered across the Indian's chest as he closed in on me. Flipping backwards, Mohawk landed face down in the dirt squirming from the shock of the blast. Rufus, not normally a vicious dog, worked feverishly nipping and snarling at Scar Lip who still seemed to be recovering from the blow I had delivered with the tire thumper.

"Rufus," I called as I spun to my left and fired the second round at Scar Lip. The impact of the rock salt knocked the demon sideways causing his feet to trip over one another, and he sprawled across the ground.

Suddenly a large hand grabbed my arm, and I found myself being spun around to face the bloodied body of Mohawk. Yanking me toward him he punched me in the nose. My eyes watered as pain wracked my face for a second time. I think the bastard would have broke my neck had it not been for Rufus who leaped upward and sank his teeth into the man's fist.

Releasing his grip on me, Mohawk turned to the dog. In the next few seconds everything seemed to blur. Rufus leaped backward and let go of Mohawk who then pursued him. Scar Lip, rising once again from the dirt, staggered toward me, and I noticed a whirlwind spinning across the ground. As it engulfed Elsa's twisted remains I skipped backward in a state of panic. It was then that I noticed the dust whirling about my own feet.

Adrenaline roared through my veins like rocket fuel as I dashed forward and leaped up into the cab of the semi. As I yanked the door shut behind me I was relieved to see the dissipating whirlwind continue past the vehicle and sink into the ground.

One of those things *almost got me!* I released the air brakes and slammed the truck into gear.

"Rufus!" I screamed as I tromped down on the gas and released the clutch, and the big rig lurched forward. The scowling face of Scar

Lip appeared in my window as he launched himself up and clung to the driver side mirror. Standing on the sideboard of my rig, he began punching and clawing at my face through the open window. Unable to do anything else I bit down hard on the hand that gripped my face and swung my own fist repeatedly in retaliation. I delivered several blows to Scar Lip's face before his grip broke free, and he lost his bid to remain on the step. He slammed into to the ground and tumbled away from the rolling tires before rising once again to his feet.

As I glanced into my side mirror the sight of a third demon rising up from Elsa's remains sickened me. To my horror, as I passed the corner of the house, I saw Maria step out of the other house.

She's done for.

Turning my gaze from the side mirror to the road before me, I wrenched the wheel and turned the rig through a portion of the cotton field. I struggled with the rough earth before wrestling the vehicle over several bumps and steering it onto the paved roadway. Panic gripped me when I spotted the third warrior, naked but for a portion of Elsa's shirt and the pouch around his neck, squatting precariously on the rear fender of the tanker-trailer. His large black eyes were focused on my image in the mirror. Running close behind were Scar Lip, Mohawk, and now a fourth warrior that I guessed had been conjured from what was left of Maria.

The instinct for survival overcame the nearly immobilizing fear that wracked my nerves, and I began steering wildly, swerving back and forth, in an attempt to throw the demon from the tanker-trailer. Focusing on a utility pole on the opposite side of the road, I timed my steering before raking the length of the tanker down the side of the pole. Wood splintered from the pole. When the steel ladder collided with the shaft the truck lurched, and the pole shifted, snapping the power lines attached to it and sending an explosion of sparks into the air.

My vehicle rocked, its wheels momentarily slipping into the shallow culvert, before coming back onto the shoulder of the road. Struggling to steady the truck and keep it from veering out into the field of cotton to my left, I pulled hard on the wheel. All the while I continued watching the mirrors for any sign of the demon that had now completely disappeared from my view. I gained control of the rig and peered at the roadway behind the truck as I swerved back to the right side of the roadway. I didn't see him anywhere.

I stomped down on the accelerator pedal with all the pressure I could muster while my white-knuckled hands gripped the wheel. Wanting to put as much distance as possible between the truck and the three runners who continued to pursue me, I drove.

A howl that made my blood run cold erupted from the passenger side of the truck as the door swung open. Instinctively, I snatched up the steel bar next to my seat. As the half-naked demon leaped upward I swung the makeshift club catching him square in the face as he entered the rig. The bastard faltered, and I swerved causing the door to slam hard on his knees as he lay halfway into the cab, sprawled across the seat. Clawing at the wheel with one hand, he dug the bony, claw-like fingers of his other hand into my right leg.

His fingertips drove deep into my thigh like steel pins, and I roared in pain as I fought to shake him loose. Cutting back with the wheel, the door slung open just as I brought the pipe down on his head. Blood oozed from the resulting gash, and he stared dazedly up at me with his large, dark eyes. Releasing his grip, the demon slipped backward as a third blow struck him solidly on the top of the head. His howl became a moan.

Fighting to stay conscious, the demon retreated. I swerved slightly just as I struck him one, last, definitive blow. He lurched backward and slammed into the door just as it swung inward. Tumbling downward, striking the step on the fuel tank before slamming into the ground, he rolled and bounced out into the lush, green field of cotton growing alongside the roadway.

"Shit! How the hell did he get up here?" I asked, grimacing as I glanced at the bloody wound in my leg. It occurred to me that he must have traversed the length of the vehicle by climbing along the undercarriage. No small feat in my estimation.

Gaining speed, and losing sight of the other demons, I drove maybe four miles or so before the pain in my nose and thigh became too intense to ignore. Feeling a bit faint, I glanced down and realized my pant leg was soaked with blood, and I feared that if the wound went unattended I was gonna bleed to death. Taking a quick look in the side mirrors, I searched for any sign of the dust devils. Seeing nothing, I pulled over to the side of the highway and parked.

The first thing I did was lean out the open window and look directly into the mirror. Grasping my nose and clamping it securely between two fingers, I jerked it back to the right and felt it snap into place. Tears welled up and poured down my face as I let out a sharp cry. Having busted my nose in high school I'd learned the nasty little trick of resetting it from my football coach. Right then my face hurt something awful, but I was confident that my nose was back in the right place. Wiping the tears from my cheeks I was thankful that I always carried a first aid kit. I opened the door and stepped down from the running board, and with little effort I forced my arm behind the seat. I found the kit with no trouble and pulled the metal box from its catch mounted on the rear wall.

Looking once more at my thigh I realized my pants were going to have to come down if I was going to clean and bandage the leg, so I closed the door and limped around to the other side of the truck. As I worked I kept looking down the road for any sign of those demon bastards. Shielding myself from any passersby, not that there was much traffic on the road, I backed up to the side of the rig, lowered my trousers, and took a good look at the scratches. The wounds looked deep and were bleeding more than I liked. I figured they needed stitches for sure, but for now a tight bandage was about the best I could provide. Breaking open the kit, I tore open a gauze pad soaked in hydrogen peroxide and daubed at the deep gouges.

"Shit," I yelped as the liquid struck open flesh. Working quickly, I taped several dry, mesh pads to the claw marks. Satisfied, I pulled up my pants, tucked in my shirt and buckled my belt.

I stood there for a moment, trembling and wondering if I was losing my mind. Panic gripped me, and I trembled as tears streamed down my face. I sobbed as the full force of everything that had happened started to weigh on me. The fear, the deaths, and the pain my

Momma had suffered, and the stress of being accused of the crimes all bore down on me in that single instant. I don't know how long I leaned there in the shadow of the tanker before I finally regained my composure. Slowly, I pulled myself back together and wiped the remnants of tears on the sleeve of my shirt before staring off into space for what seemed an eternity. When I regained my senses I decided to go to Billy Don and talk to him about everything that had happened.

I stepped away from the shadows of the tanker and turned toward the running board to close up the kit. I'd barely snapped the lid closed when I heard the sound of panting and abruptly became aware that something was approaching me from underneath the tanker.

Reaching up, I wrenched the door open and lunged into the cab after my steel tire thumper. As I turned to face the demon I was relieved to see Rufus. His lathered coat shone in the sunlight and his long, pink tongue hung from his panting mouth.

"Rufus, you about scared the shit out of me. What the hell are you doing here?"

The dog whined a little, shaking. Seeing his owners murdered must've been confusing at best for the poor boy. The truck and I must have been the only thing familiar to him.

"I can't believe you followed me all the way here." He sought my hands, and I rubbed his head trying to soothe him as best I could. "I guess they scared the hell out of you too, huh, old boy? Well, you're safe for now, I hope." I glanced down the roadway warily. "You better come with me, and I'll figure out what to do with you later."

Noticing a tear in the side of the seat cushion, I thought about the telephone pole I'd hit during my escape. "Come on," I said to Rufus as I tossed the medical kit up into the cab and closed the door. "Let's go take a look at the damage." Together, we sauntered around the front of the semi to the driver side of the vehicle.

I looked at the ruined paint on the fender of the cab, the twisted ladder, and the scars on the tanker caused by raking the utility pole. "Shit." My eyes took in the minor scrapes going all the way back to the rear of the truck. I wasn't happy about having to explain it to Billy but was relieved that it wasn't worse. Then something caught my eye.

Looking back down the highway, across the great expanse of the open prairie toward the distant horizon, I saw black smoke rising from the direction of the Morales place. I thought back to the store at Ten Mile Fork and realized the devils had torched the place.

"What in the *hell* are they?" I spat as I pondered the appearance of the three additional warriors. It also occurred to me that they had a curious desire to hide evidence of their crimes, as well as their own existence, and to kill anyone who might have seen their transformation. A gust of wind broke me from my musing and made me look around worried that they had gotten close. I'd seen those little whirlwinds all my life, but I'd never been frightened of them like I was now.

"Murdering bastards. That's what they are for sure, Rufus." I scratched the old dog behind the ears and stared for a moment longer at the distant plume of smoke.

"I better get this thing back to the shed," I told Rufus, thinking I should head on over to Billy's place and face the music. Besides, I wasn't about to finish my lease runs in the state of mind I was in. I knew the police would put this one together in a hurry, and I didn't want them telling Billy before I got a chance to explain. I doubted I could tell the police what really happened and had a feeling they were going to be real interested in either questioning me or arresting me.

I opened the door and managed to get my arms around Rufus to lift him up into the cab. He hesitated a moment before bounding across the cab and parking himself in the passenger seat.

I stole a glance backward at the billowing smoke. For a moment, I could have sworn I saw four men not too far off in the distance approaching me down the roadway. Their forms shimmered in the heat of the warming pavement, twisting their bodies into a ghastly mirage. Anxiety ripped through me, and I scooted up into the cab of the truck and slammed it into gear. With repeated glances in my rearview mirror the dog and I made our way back to Levelland.

Arriving in town just before noon, I drove directly to the South Plains Office Park and slipped inside the dentist office where Melissa worked as a hygienist. The receptionist paged her on the intercom and was told that she was with a patient and would come to the lobby when she was finished. I waited patiently knowing she went to lunch from noon until around one and would be out pretty soon. Sure enough, Melissa appeared just a few minutes after twelve.

"Brady, what are you doing here?" she asked, a bright smile gleaming beneath her sparkling blue eyes.

"I need a little help." Her eyes followed mine when I looked down at my thigh. Her expression said it all as we walked out of the lobby and stepped out under the midday sun.

"Damn, Brady. What have you done to yourself now?"

"Well…"

"Yeah, okay. You're covering for another friend, right?" She unlocked her car and opened the driver side door.

"No. But I can't really explain it just now. I'm sorry to have to ask during your lunch break, but I'm hoping you might patch me up."

Shaking her head she tossed her purse into her car and put one hand on her hip. "Yeah, you know I will, but you're worrying me. I'm starting to believe you're in some kind of trouble. These sort of wounds ain't normal, Brady."

"Yeah, I know," I said, unable to offer any further explanation.

"Well, get in. I'll do this, but you really ought to be going to a doctor."

"I'll follow you in the truck."

"Alright. I'll see you at the house."

I followed her across town and left Rufus in the air-conditioned cab while I went inside the house. It took her a while to gather what she needed, but after a rather painful thirty minutes I left her house with my wounds stitched up and fresh pads beneath my elastic bandage. I promised to take her to dinner, and she made me promise to behave myself and stop doing whatever it was that was getting me hurt. With a quick peck on her lips I assured her that this was the last time I would come to her for medical attention and quickly made my way out.

I made a quick trip to Walmart and bought a new pair of jeans changing out of the bloodied ones in the cab of my truck outside the store. Stashing the old jeans behind the seat, I headed across town.

Ten minutes later I pulled through the gate of the chain link fence and into the staging yard behind Billy Don's ranch-style brick house. His rig was in the yard, so I figured he wasn't out making runs today. He only hauled when someone was out or when the workload was too heavy for the crew to complete in a timely manner. All the trucks belonged to Billy Don, so maintenance and repairs went through his service contract at Skip's Big Truck Repair Shop.

Knowing he wouldn't want the truck running around banged up like it was, I decided it would be best to get the repairs scheduled immediately. But, first, I wanted to talk to Billy. At that moment I was concerned about my relationship with him and needed to set things straight.

"Rufus, you stay here. We'll get this over with and then I'll get us something to eat," I said, rubbing the dog on the forehead and gently patting his muzzle.

Stepping down from the rig, I crossed the parking lot and knocked on the back door to the house. Lilly Jean, Billy's wife, answered the door with a look of concern on her face. A small woman with blue eyes and blond hair styled short, Lilly's face was adorned with makeup and a complimentary shade of bright red lipstick. She wore Western-cut dress slacks, a frilly blouse and a pair of brightly polished cowboy boots. With a forced smile, she pushed the storm door open allowing a draft of cool conditioned air to strike me. "Brady, are you alright?" Lilly asked, her face betraying her repulsion for the appearance of my bruised face.

"Hi, Miss Lilly. Yes, I'm okay. I just need to talk to Billy." Billy Don called her Miss Lilly, and all of us simply followed suit.

"I'm sorry, Brady, but he's gone on over to Lubbock. I expect him back in time for supper."

"Oh. I saw his pickup and the semi here, so I thought he was home."

"Yes, he took my Saab in for service."

"I tried calling him on his cell phone earlier, but it went to voicemail."

"He had some other errands to run and a doctor's appointment, so maybe he's in a bad spot for reception. You might try him again."

"All right. Sorry to bother you, Miss Lilly. I'll get a hold of him. Thanks."

"No bother, Brady. You have a nice day, now." Lilly Jean said nodding before retreating into the house and allowing the door to close. The way she'd looked at me, the way her eyes had gone a little wide, cut me. Was she actually afraid of me?

I guess she probably doesn't know what to think of me now, with all the shit that's happened, I thought as I turned and headed back to the truck. Once inside, I dialed Billy's cell phone number again but got his voicemail. I hung up. What I needed to say would be best said directly.

I called my house to check on my mother but got the same response there. I figured she was over at Caroline's, or maybe she had gone over to Sophia's house. Knowing it best to go on over to Skip's and get and estimate on the damage I shifted the rig into gear.

I left the yard and made my way to the garage located a few blocks away. Skip's Big Truck Repair Shop was a long, rectangular, building with four bays and an office on one end. Parts and general storage were located in the windowless section at the end of the building opposite the office and beyond the bays. Each of the bays sported a garage door at either end to allow trucks to pull through. Light filtered into the office end of the building through a large plate-glass window and steel-framed glass door that led into a small customer lobby that sported some magazines, plastic chairs, and a few vending machines. Pulling off the street and parking near the office end of the building, I leaped down from the cab and headed into the office.

"Hey, Brake. How you doin' today?"

It's was easier to lie than to tell the truth. I slid my shaking, nerve wracked hands into the pockets on the front of my jeans and looked at the dark complexioned Ruby Brown, whose brown eyes peered up at me from behind the service desk and then looked askance to avoid the bruising on my face. "Ah, I'm okay, Ruby. Is Skippy around?"

She must have seen that I wasn't my jovial self. Ruby turned away, returning her gaze to the computer screen as she lifted the telephone receiver to her mouth. "Skip, please report to the service desk." Her voice rang loudly from a series of speakers throughout the building and the lot outside. "Skip, please report to the service desk."

"Thanks, Ruby."

"Yeah, not a problem."

I twitched impatiently and paced the small waiting room suddenly feeling a bit lightheaded. I searched my pockets for some cash. Discovering two one-dollar bills I fed them into a vending machine and hit the D4 button. I watched with hungry anticipation as the coiled wire turned, and my chocolate bar slipped over the edge of the shelf and fell into the vacant trough below. Pushing the panel back into the machine I retrieved the candy and tore open the wrapper.

Like a ravished survivor of some terrible tragedy I stuffed the entire bar into my mouth and chewed voraciously as I choked it down. Just as I swallowed the last gob of the chocolate I spotted Skip cutting across the back lot and heading toward the office. I could tell by the look on his face he was upset about something, or maybe he was just annoyed at being paged. Wrenching the back door open he walked into the office and stalked into the service area behind the counter.

"What's up, Ruby?" he growled. The grimace on his annoyed face changed only slightly when he spotted me leaning on the service counter. "Hey, Brake. Jesus, what the hell happened to your face?"

"Brake is 'what's up'. He wanted to see you," Ruby responded, her tone sour and sarcastic.

"Well, here I am," he spat back.

"Hey, Skip. I'm here because I had a little accident, and I'd like you to give me an estimate so I can give it to Billy. I'm fixin' to head back over to his place shortly, and I'd like to have it in hand if that works for you."

I guess he could tell from the tone of my voice that I was none too happy. His demeanor changed for the better, and Skip grabbed a clipboard off the end of the counter, stepping out into the customer area. "Yeah, sure, let's go take a quick look at it."

Moments later, Skip was standing next to my truck scribbling on the estimate form clamped to the clipboard. "Damn, Brakesy, what the hell did you do to that ladder?"

"Ahh, I clipped me a pole this morning. Long story."

"This morning or on the way home last night from Cactus Creek?" he asked with a sly grin.

"No, this morning."

"And what about you, buddy, did you get jumped or something? You look like you been in a fight with a pro boxer. You okay?"

"Ah no, this happened when I messed up the truck. I'm fine. It'll be fine."

I stepped out of the way as a pickup truck with the garage logo emblazoned on the side door approached from the back lot. Ruby waved at me as she drove by and turned onto the street. Skip didn't seem to notice her.

"Boy howdy, looks like you ran the whole side of the truck into it. Look at your mirror."

"Shit." I hadn't really noticed the mirror frame. It had gotten twisted a little at some point during the ordeal. Memory of the demon hanging onto the frame came to mind although I suspected it happened when I raked the rest of the truck down the utility pole.

Rufus yelped and whined a little from the cab of the truck as we walked across in front of the rig and around to the other side. "That your dog, Brakesy? Didn't know you had a dog."

"Yeah, well I don't. I'm just watching him for a friend."

"Damn! You scraped the entire length of the truck down that pole, didn't ya? And what the heck is that spattered all over the side of the tanker there? Looks kinda like rust, or paint, or something."

I didn't feel much like talking, and I sure as hell had no desire to discuss the swath of blood despite the fact that a coat of dust had dulled the redness of it. It seemed like a whole lot more blood than I remembered seeing earlier, so I didn't respond.

Standing silently as the minutes ticked by, either my nerves were beginning to calm or the chocolate was performing its magic because I began to feel normal again. Skip finally stopped scribbling on his pad and darted toward the office.

"Okay! Give me a minute and I'll have this printed up for you," he drawled.

Following him across the lot to the front of the building, we entered the office where I again waited patiently. But that, the patience part, became near impossible as I watched a Levelland police cruiser pull into the driveway, and drive slowly past my rig. My nerves began to twitch, and sweat beaded quickly on my forehead despite the coolness of the air-conditioned lobby. Anxious to go I leaned on the counter, momentarily taking my eye off the cruiser to look back at Skip who was pounding away on his computer keyboard.

Gazing through the window once more, I was relieved to see the police car had driven around back and had not stopped to inspect my vehicle.

"It's gonna take me a few minutes, Brake. I got to enter this shit myself, and I don't type worth a damn. Damn that, Ruby! She's always runnin' off and doing something other than being here in the office."

"Well, Junior, that's why you ought to hire a runner so we don't have to send her all over the place to pick shit up," offered Gus Johnson as he swept through the interior door from the shop and crossed over to the soda machine near the couch.

Gus was an older man, late fifties, tall, slender, dark skin with graying hair cropped close to his scalp. His thick, dark-rimmed glasses gave him a scholarly look, though he'd never done anything but work on trucks. He'd been working at the truck center since Skip senior hired him more than thirty years ago. I like Gus. He's a straight shooter, and he knows more about trucks than any three of the other mechanics combined.

Skip continued to punch away at the keyboard with an intensified fervor and didn't respond.

"What you doin' in here, Brakesy?"

"Hey, Gus. Oh, just getting an estimate on some work. Hit a pole this morning."

"Damn, that your rig yonder?" He stared out through the window at the damaged vehicle. "It looks as though it had the same run in as your face."

"Yeah, in a way it did," I replied, thinking the old man never seemed to miss an opportunity to take a crack at somebody.

"Don't look that bad." A grin formed on his face. "The truck that is. I bet Billy Don was right pissed about it, weren't he?"

"He doesn't know yet. But I suspect he'll be right pissed about it for sure."

"Here you go, Brake," Skip announced, rising from his chair at the rear of the office and walking toward the service counter.

It was at that moment that a siren wailed in front of the building, and I turned to see several local police cars and a County Sheriff's cruiser along with two Texas Highway Patrol vehicles sweep into the yard effectively surrounding the building with their lights flashing. Roaring to a halt, the officers leaped out of their cars, some with guns drawn, and they charged at the building.

"What the hell?" Skip yelped, gawking out the window at the circus that had just set up camp in his parking lot.

"They lookin' for you, Brake?" Gus asked quietly.

"I reckon so," I said. "Yep, I reckon so."

❄ 5 ❄

Where are the Morales, Mr. Drake? You killed that poor man, his wife, and their daughter-in-law and set their homes on fire, didn't you." Sheriff Baker snarled, his finger pointing at me inches from my face. "I know you did it. Why don't you just own up to it?"

"Because it's bullshit!" I replied, unnerved. "I ain't never killed nobody."

"We saw your fuckin' tire prints in the sand. It's the same pattern you left at Ten Mile Fork two days earlier. We know you were there, Brady. The assignment log at Smith Oil Transport confirms it, and Mrs. Smith said you arrived there about noon all nervous and bruised. You struggled with those folks, killed them all, and burned them out, didn't you!" Sergeant Dickens shouted.

"No. I told you, I don't know anything about that."

"Let's all take a clarifying look at this for a minute, Mr. Drake. We found the burnt remains of one man. Four more are missing and presumably dead all within days of each other. And you were at both crime scenes about the same time these events happened. But, in your almighty arrogance, you expect us to believe that you know absolutely *nothing* about either incident and weren't involved? Bullshit, Mr. Drake? Oh yes, I agree that's bullshit!"

"Sheriff Baker, I don't have to listen to this shit. I've done nothing wrong, and all this questioning ain't going to make me tell you anything different."

"You *do* have to listen! Mister Drake. And you're going to tell us what we want to know or your ass is going to jail!" Sergeant Dickens growled, glaring hard at me from across the table.

I was sitting in a plastic chair inside the break room of Skip's Big Truck Repair Shop staring back at the accusing glares of local, county, and state police officers. We'd been going at this for over an hour under the drop-panel ceiling and fluorescent lights, and I wasn't giving an inch. To my way of thinking if I started down the road to telling them exactly what I had witnessed they'd lock me up for psychological observation and try me for murder to boot. If I continued to tell them nothing; they had nothing but suspicions and circumstances. I'd watched enough television and read enough about the law to know they couldn't hold me without hard evidence.

"Where is the Morales family, and why did you burn down their house?" Sheriff Baker was back in my face, his eyes glaring at me hotly.

"And why is your truck all wrecked up along with your face?" added Deputy Dawson from his place by the door.

"Your leg don't look none too healthy. What happened there?" the third officer, Sergeant Dickens, added to the barrage, looking at me like he could see horns growing out my head or something.

I looked down and saw that a three-inch spot of blood had seeped through the pant leg of my jeans. Hell, I hadn't even felt a thing. But adrenaline will do that to you.

"I'm telling you, for the hundredth time, I don't know anything about any missing people or whatever else the hell happened. I rejected that load of oil at the Morales place and went on to my next job. I got distracted and hit a utility pole. That's the whole of it."

"And the dog? How the hell did you end up with the Morales's dog?" Dickens asked.

That one made me sweat a bit because any answer was likely to sound phony. But I figured the truth wouldn't hurt so long as I started where I came up with the dog. "He followed me, I guess. I don't know why. But when I stopped to assess the damage from my little jaunt off the edge of the road he showed up. I knew he was Hector's dog, so I picked him up. I figured I'd take him back down there tonight after I get off work."

"You were going to take your *own* time to drive him nearly *sixty miles*, tonight when you were less than a few miles from the place when he showed up?" Dickens questioned doubtfully.

"Yeah, that's right. Hector and his wife are my friends. I figured I'd pay them a visit and return the dog."

"That's bullshit, Drake. Fucking bullshit. People don't kill their friends. You killed those poor folks and burned their bodies inside those houses. And then, in your twisted mind, you just suddenly thought you'd like to have their dog. You're a sick, murdering bastard and you know it."

"That's not true, Sergeant Dickens, and from where I sit it don't look like you have a shred of evidence to prove anything. I'm tired of this crap. Now are you going to charge me with something? Because if you're not I want to go home."

"You'll go home when we get the truth," Sheriff Baker snapped.

Standing, I glared back at him. "Then charge me and let me call a lawyer. Otherwise, I'm leaving."

"Sit down."

My nerves twitching like a nervous rattlesnake I strolled toward the exit. Deputy Dawson's outstretched hand pressed firmly on the door in front of me. I looked him in the eye as I spoke. "Sheriff, you want to call off Deputy Dawg-son here, or shall I file charges of false imprisonment?"

"You're going to slip up, Drake, and when you do we'll be there. We're going to get you, and I pray we do before you kill anyone else," Sheriff Baker replied, making a gesture toward the deputy. Deputy Dawson's hand fell away, and I jerked the door open before stepping into the waiting area.

Gus, Skip, and Ruby all stood behind the counter their eyes wide looking at me.

"Later ya'll." I nodded and walked out of the building.

With my estimate tucked securely in the back pocket of my denim jeans, I leaped up into the cab of the truck. I took a moment and scratched Rufus around the ears before I started the rig. For whatever reason I realized that the police hadn't noticed the blood spattered down the length of the tanker. If they had they would've had enough evidence to hold me. Mixed with the dust from the road I guessed it looked more like rust than blood, and in their anxious mood to interrogate me they had ignored it.

Fifteen minutes later, I ordered two Sonic burger specials, one for me and one for the dog, at the Sonic on College Avenue in Levelland. When a cute little college girl delivered the order to my truck I thanked her before Rufus and I ate lunch.

They probably didn't think I saw them, but across the street sat a Levelland Police cruiser. They dogged me the rest of the afternoon until I lit out of town.

❊ 6 ❊

That's a pile of horse shit!" Billy Don croaked and released cigarette smoke into the air above the booth where we all sat huddled over the table.

I took a sip of my second Lone Star and set the mug down as I spoke quietly, not wanting to be overheard. "Yup, I had a feeling you'd say that. That's why I didn't tell you bastards. Hell, I wouldn't believe it if one of you were telling me, so I don't expect any of you to believe me. But that's what the hell is going on whether you believe it or not."

"Out of a freakin' whirlwind? How the hell could that happen?" Red McCauley shook his head scoffing quietly as he took another sip of his beer.

"I don't know if I believe this whirlwind stuff. We've all seen these things and ain't never seen nothin' the likes of what you're talking about. I don't doubt you saw some murdering bastards doing bad shit. Maybe they're using some kind of magic trick to throw you off or somethin'. But why? I mean it sounds to me like they're following you, Brady. Why do you think that is?" Jimmy John leaned back in his seat eyeing me with suspicion written all over his face.

"Ain't nobody followin' him, for Christ's sake." Billy Don grumbled tipping back his third shot of whiskey and following it with the last swallow from his seventh beer of the evening. With a snap of his fingers Billy Don signaled the barmaid to bring him another round. "Brady, just tell us the goddamned truth, and stop all this bullshit. We can't help ya if you don't come clean. You know damn well we'll stand by ya, but you've got to level with us. I don't give a damn about the damage to the truck. My insurance will cover that. What *does* concern me are all the goddamned people coming up missing and the fires and all. Brady, that bullshit has got to come to a halt! Now you level with us. And I don't want you repeatin' this horse shit about whirlwinds and dust devils and all that. I want what *really* happened, and then I'll get you a damn good lawyer and the best psychologist money can buy."

"Billy," I said, shaking my head, struggling to respond to his assumptions, "I *am* leveling with you. You just ain't hearing me."

"You're a goddamned liar!" he snarled causing several of the other patrons to look over at our huddled group and nearly making the waitress drop his order as she reached in and set it on the table before him.

"Ah, to hell with this. I'm going home." I poured the last three swallows of beer down my throat. Feeling frustrated, I just wanted get into my truck and head down the highway. The road has always been a good place for me. Nothing clears my head like barreling down an open stretch of highway with the radio on and the window open.

"Hey, don't run off on us, Brakesy. The evening is young yet! I think you're about as crazy as a rabid coyote, but I want to hear a bit more about all this." Red tipped back a shot of bourbon obviously enjoying the banter. I realized that none of them probably believed me and, deep down, I couldn't blame them.

"I need some air. Besides, Momma's home alone, and she'll probably feel a whole lot better if she knows I'm close by."

"Don't bother comin' in tomorrow morning. Your truck's in the fuckin' shop, and I can't have you running the roads until you get your goddamned facts straight," Billy Don grumbled at me, staring me down from across the booth.

"Yeah, fine," I replied, rising to my feet. "I need a couple days off anyway. And, Billy," I said without giving it any real thought, "you've had way too many brews. You wouldn't know the facts if they punched you in the face."

Billy Don slid off the end of the bench knocking his mug off the table and sending it crashing to the floor where it exploded. Beer sprayed ten feet in every direction covering everything in its path with foam. Despite the country music belting out of the jukebox and the din of three-dozen voices all trying to be heard every head in the Cactus Creek Saloon turned in our direction.

"Don't take that fuckin' attitude with me, Brady." Billy rocked unsteadily on his feet jabbing at my face with a finger. Spittle flew from his mouth as he spoke. "I ain't the one runnin' around the country-side killing people."

"You're crossing the damn line now, Billy. You might want to shut the hell up before you lose my respect," I said, feeling the heat rise up within me and knowing every pair of eyes and ears were turned our way.

"Respect! You get respect when you give it. Using my rig to run about committing crimes ain't any sign of respect, so what more could I lose? You're just like your old man."

"Billy, that's enough, damn it!" Red grabbed Billy Don's outstretched arm, forcing his finger away from my face.

It took every ounce of will I possessed to resist punching Billy Don in the face. Instead, I turned and strode out of the saloon. J.J. followed me, stopping momentarily to toss enough money on the bar to cover his tab.

Despite the fact it was cooler inside than out it felt like I stepped from an oven into a winter night as I stormed out of the Cactus Creek Saloon. This whole thing was beginning to disturb me something awful. Shaking off the accusing looks of the other patrons I pulled my cap off my head and wiped the sweat from my brow.

Rufus spotted me and leaped up from underneath Billy Don's pickup truck where he had been napping. The dog sauntered over to me, and I ruffled the fur about his ears, and he sat still by my side.

"Don't let him get to you, Brady," J.J. said, as he followed me out of the saloon. "You know he can be a hothead. He's had way too much to drink, and he don't believe half of what he's saying."

"That may be, J.J., but I can't listen to any more of it right now."

I could see the concern in his eyes as I looked at my friend. J.J. was my closest friend. Until he married Felicia Lopez, we were insepa-rable. These days, we spent evenings after work at the saloon and occasionally grabbed our gear on Sunday to go fishing up along the Red River.

"Well, as messed up as it sounds, I think you're caught up in some weird shit. You've got to admit it's all kind of hard to believe given what you told us. But I don't think for a minute you'd come up with a story as screwed up as this if you were trying to cover up murdering people," J.J. said with a half grin on his face.

I looked at my old friend as I stepped down off the front porch of the saloon and realized he was doing his best to console me. "Thanks, Jay."

"It's nothing," he replied. "How you getting home? You need a ride?"

I then remembered having ridden here with Billy Don. I'd met Billy at his house and rode over here with him. Now my only mode of transportation was my own two feet. I turned back to Jay.

"Come to think of it I reckon I need a ride," I said, trying to smile.

J.J. nodded and, together, we strode over to his truck. Rufus leaped up through open gate and lay down on the bed of the Chevy Silverado pickup, and we were on our way. As we headed toward Broken Spoke, I gave J.J. as many answers as he had questions. Shaking his head and cursing in disbelief he said little else. I know he wanted to believe me. Reaching the outskirts of Broken Spoke, we turned off the highway and made our way down East Street toward my house. I tensed immediately when I spotted a black sedan with government plates parked on the side of the street in front of my home and two men in dark dress suits standing on the porch talking to Momma. She had a perplexed expression on her face as she stood behind the screen door.

"Who the hell is that?"

"I don't know, Jay, but I'm sure fixin' to find out."

"You need me to stay?" he said, stopping the truck and slipping the shift handle into neutral.

"No, I best handle this on my own. Thanks for the ride. I'll catch up to you later. Give your pretty little wife a kiss for me."

"Okay, Brady. Ya'll take care, and call me if you need anything."

"Thanks, J.J.," I said, shoving the door closed behind me. Turning toward the house I strode across the lawn with Rufus on my heels.

As I approached I kept my eyes trained on the two men. They must have heard me because they turned towards me when I got close.

"Brady Drake?" asked the tall, red haired man. He was dressed in a black suit, black shoes, a white shirt, and gray tie and flashed his identification. "I'm agent Wilson O'Reilly from the Federal Bureau of Investigation. This here is Ben Swift, special detective with the Bureau of Indian Affairs and a tribal policeman from Pine Ridge, South Dakota," he stated as the other man waved a wallet bearing a shield and identification.

Detective Ben Swift, also about six feet tall, extended his hand and grasped mine. He had a swarthy complexion, and his dark hair was cropped neatly. He was rugged looking, and his sharp features were probably considered handsome by those of the female persuasion. The man was wearing a black suit similar to the one worn by the FBI agent and a string tie held together with a small clasp in the shape of a Lakota war shield. Saying nothing he shook my hand with a firm grip peering intensely into my eyes. His manner was direct, suggesting his desire to get on with whatever business it was they were here to conduct.

"What's this all about?" I acknowledged their credentials and released the detective's hand.

"It's about the man that came here and killed Donny," Momma said before backing away from the door and vanishing into the house.

"Might we come in or go somewhere we can talk in private?" O'Reilly asked.

"Yeah, why don't ya'll come on inside." I walked past them and stepped into the house. Not used to having a dog, I forgot Rufus and he wound up staying outside on the porch.

O'Reilly closed the door after following me inside, and I gestured with my hand for the two men to have a seat in any of the three armchairs facing the broken television. O'Reilly settled himself into one, but Swift remained standing near the door.

"Your mother tells us her attacker had large, dark eyes and may have been of Native American descent. Do you know, or have you seen, anyone of that description?" O'Reilly asked.

"No," I replied.

"Mr. Drake, it's very important that you confide in us if you've had any interaction with anyone who fits this description. I assure you that we intend to see that no further harm comes to your mother, or to you, but we have to be sure of what it is we're dealing with. Now, again Mr. Drake, have you any knowledge of anyone matching this description? Or have you seen anything out of the ordinary? Something that you can't explain?" The Pine Ridge detective crossed his arms, giving me a long look.

It was the detective's last question that caused me to pause and consider that maybe these men *did* know something about what I had been going through.

"Maybe," I drawled, my tone guarded. "How would you know anything about it?"

O'Reilly sat perched on the edge of the recliner and flashed a smile as he accepted a glass of lemonade from a tray in my mother's hands. "Thank you, ma'am," he said then turned his focus on me. "Mr. Drake, I work in a special investigations unit for the FBI. The cases we are involved in usually exhibit abnormalities that make them difficult to solve. Swift is a special investigator for the Tribal Police at Pine Ridge Indian Reservation and part of a law enforcement arm of the Bureau of Indian Affairs. The Bureau and Swift have been working together for well over a year on a very difficult case that we think might be related to the man who attacked your mother."

Swift nodded acknowledging both O'Reilly's words and my mother as he, too, accepted a glass of the cold beverage. "Thanks, Mom," I said, as I took the last glass from the tray. Looking back at O'Reilly I opened my mouth but quickly clamped it shut when Swift spoke.

"We've been following a group of men from two reservations in South Dakota. They're elusive, but we know they're here. We happened to catch a local news report about the incident down at Ten Mile Fork, and, after contacting Texas Highway Patrol for further details, we suspect your case is linked to these same men."

As he laid it out to me I had a notion that they were off track. What I had experienced didn't seem likely to have anything to do with a group of men from South Dakota. "I didn't see any group of men. I mean, I saw a group, but…"

"I know," Swift interjected. "You saw something indescribable. But, for the benefit of clarification, can you tell us what it is you saw?"

I was reluctant to say anything, but Swift's reference to 'something indescribable' made me feel like he might actually have a chance at believing me. And, looking into his eyes, I sensed something in him might know what it was that I had seen. I sipped my lemonade and fidgeted in my chair for a moment before finally deciding to give it a go. *Well, I'm going to have to tell someone, and at least they're not here threatening to arrest me.*

"The police are trying to pin murder and arson charges on me, but they have no idea what I've seen. And I haven't told them the whole story because I don't think anyone will believe what I saw. Besides, I ain't real sure *I* believe what I saw, and I ain't interested in ending up in the loony bin."

I rocked on the edge of my seat for a minute sipping my lemonade and trying to gather my thoughts. "Detective Swift, I get a feeling you might know something about what I saw, so I'm gonna take a chance and lay it out straight." I turned my head toward the kitchen and called out, "Momma, I'm sorry I haven't told you before, but you're gonna want to hear this."

My mother lurked in the shadows of the dimly lit kitchen, smoking a cigarette and listening. "What have you seen, Brady?" my mother asked, her voice was hushed and hung in the air as she waited for a response.

"Does what you saw have anything to do with whirlwinds?" Swift asked?

I was stunned by the question, but almost overjoyed as I recognized the implications of what he'd said. "Yes, yes it does! I can't believe ya'll know about that," I answered excitedly. The words flowed out of me like I was allowed to breathe after near suffocation. For the next twenty minutes I told them almost all that I had experienced at Ten Mile Fork and at the Morales lease and then about the attack on my mother. The two lawmen sipped quietly on their drinks listening to my every word. "And I'm some worried that they'll show up here again and hurt my mom. Or kill her."

"Brady, you knew about this man, this *thing*, that came here and attacked me? Why didn't you tell the police?" Momma said, her voice torn between disbelief and anger.

"I'm sorry, Momma. I was scared they might haul me away, and I was concerned about your safety if I was locked up." I felt as though I'd somehow betrayed her. And my guilt redoubled as her head drooped, and she disappeared again into the kitchen.

"Well, I think you're absolutely right to be concerned about your safety," O'Reilly interjected. "You've engaged some very dangerous men, and your lives are in danger. I think the two of you ought to accompany us to Lubbock where we'll have you sign written statements and then see to your safety. If you and your mother could relocate for a few days it might be the best thing you could do." His tone told me that he'd heard the story before and didn't believe the more outlandish parts.

"Did you take anything from any of them or know if you have a connection to any of the Indian tribes that once inhabited this area?" Swift asked.

My mind churned and I remembered the pouch I had torn off that devil's neck, the one thing I neglected to tell them. "Well, I do have a pouch I grabbed off one of 'em that ended up in my truck. I was going to destroy it but figured it might be useful somehow if the police ever arrested me."

"May we see it?" Swift asked.

"Yeah, I've got it right here," I said, slipping my fingers into my left pocket to pull the small felt bag out. "I was keeping it in my truck, but when I dropped the truck off for repairs I thought I'd best bring it along with me."

The drawstring loosened a little as I rolled it over in my hand, and an eerie feeling swept through me as the tether slid through my fingers. Swift extended his hand to me, and I gladly offered it to him.

"Padouca," Swift murmured after studying it. "Do you have any connection to the Comanche tribes that lived on this land?"

"No," I replied.

Swift ran his fingers over the stitching and quill patterns on the material, his expression thoughtful. "How many generations of your family have lived in Texas?"

"A few, I guess. In high school history we learned that most of the people in town can trace their roots back to the early days."

"His great, great grandfather settled here after a stint with the U.S. Cavalry." My mother reappeared from the kitchen, cigarette in hand. She stood in the doorway, watching us.

"He did?" I asked, looking at my mother.

"Do you know if he fought in the wars here, ma'am?"

"Yes."

"How do you know that?" I asked.

My mother looked at me with serious eyes seeming to hesitate before she answered. "I know because Walter Drake, your grandfather, used to tell stories about it." She turned her gaze back to the two lawmen. "When I was a girl dating Brady's father we often spent Sunday evenings at the Drake house. On cool evenings we sat out behind the house around a campfire and Walter Drake told stories of his grandfather. I remember him telling us that Henry Drake came to Texas as a cavalry trooper and fought against the Comanche. To have him tell it, it sounded as though it was a bloody and ruthless ordeal on both sides. I guess Henry Drake spent many years in the Army traveling all over fighting Indians. But when the Indian wars were over he settled here. That was how the Drakes came to settle in this part of Texas."

"Mom, you never told me any of this."

"Well, with the relationship being what it is between you and your father I never thought you cared to know about any of that."

"That explains much," said Swift.

"It does? How so?" I asked.

Swift shared a look with O'Reilly, who raised his hands and eyebrows before sighing and shaking his head. It seemed to me that whatever Swift was fixin' to say didn't really sit well with O'Reilly. Swift then looked directly at me. "What I'm going to tell you will be just as hard for you to believe as it was for you to tell us, and your friends, about what you saw. But, in your case, I think it may help you make sense of what you saw.

"In 1890, two Lakota warriors named Kicking Bear and Short Bull visited a Paiute Indian by the name of Wovoka. Wovoka grew up under the influence of both the Christian and Paiute religions as a boy. In his elderly years he claimed to have had a vision and to have received a message from Jesus Christ, who taught him a special dance. He then taught others and instructed them to spread the message of his return.

"People from the Nations journeyed to see Wovoka to hear his message about the rebirth of all Indians. The dance was to make the dead rise up from the earth. This great uprising would return the People and the buffalo and elk. It was said that performance of the dance would cause the earth to roll up out of itself, return balance to the sacred hoop, and bury the Europeans. Kicking Bear and Short Bull taught the dance to our people. Many called it the Circle Dance, but to the Lakota it was the Ghost Dance.

"The people had suffered much. They were desperate to return to the old ways. Dancing became their only hope and an obsession for many of the people.

"In South Dakota, reservation Indian agents Reynolds and Royer requested troops to end what they believed to be an uprising. Many of the People died. Many people did not believe in the Ghost Dance, and when the great rising did not come most of the dancing stopped."

"Now, this is not an official position held by the Bureau," O'Reilly interjected. "We believe the murders and related crimes are being perpetrated by a single group of young men. And we believe these men have ties to the reservations in South Dakota."

Swift sat silently, no expression on his face, and waited for the FBI agent to finish his comments before he continued. "A group of boys saw something that made them believe in the Ghost Dance, and as they grew they continued to secretly practice the dance and refine their approach to the ceremony. By the time they had grown into young men they had mastered the dance and learned to make it work."

"What do you mean they 'learned to make it work'? Are you saying they bring back dead people?" I stammered.

Swift leaned forward. "You're quick to catch on, Mr. Drake. They've learned to raise spirits from the dead albeit one soul at a time, sometimes two or three, but they've learned how to get results.

"And what you witnessed was a result. They're here, raising the dead, raising spirits, as they themselves have risen several times over the past one hundred years. Though it may appear to be a random act your interaction with a risen Comanche warrior is *not* a coincidence. As difficult as this is to believe it is likely the warrior you encountered was killed by your forefather or was somehow connected to him. Through the workings of the spirit world they have found you."

"Again, this is not the official position the U.S. Government is taking on this matter," O'Reilly interjected.

"And part of you, as a descendent of your forefather, is recognized by their angry and vengeful souls," the detective continued, ignoring the agent.

"That's… Fuck, that's crazy," I said, remembering my mother was in the room.

"Sounds a bit crazy, doesn't it?" O'Reilly said with a grin.

"But how is it that I could be where they were? I mean, how could they know who I was or where I was?" I stammered. "How did he find my house, and why attack my mother? It all seems kinda crazy, don't you think? Why in the hell are they here now?"

Detective Swift sipped his lemonade and waited until I sat back in my chair before he replied. It occurred to me that this man had a certain sense of timing and he did nothing, said nothing, without thinking it through. "The boys, now men and known to me as Shadow Dancers, were orphans. The result of soldiers killing their parents. They have, for the better part of over a hundred years, used this power to raise up warriors from the dead and only warriors whose passion is to kill and seek revenge. The spirit world is multidimensional, and its powers work in ways quite mysterious to the living.

"People today have a hard time believing in anything supernatural or paranormal, but that doesn't mean it doesn't exist. If you think about it, there is no way for us to detect the hundreds of radio signals flowing through our world without a radio. The spirit world is just as real, and if it didn't exist none of us would be here.

"Just imagine yourself, living multiple lives in multiple dimensions right now. Consider that these dimensions can exist in the past, present, and future, and you can see that you may have even been one of your own ancestors. What happens here affects what happens in all of the others, and vice versa. Crossing paths with the spirits of the risen was planned for you as was your workday, and the victims were just as likely to have had ties to those warriors. And Brady, not to discomfit you any more than you already are, but I feel compelled to inform you that they are after you directly."

"Oh my Lord," my mother exclaimed her hand covering her mouth and her body leaning heavily against the doorframe.

"Now folks," O'Reilly began, rising to his feet, "Swift has no way of proving any of this. It's *not* the official position of the Bureau. I think it wise not to take this theory seriously. We believe we're after some ruthless serial killers, and we'll catch them."

"They're after *me*?" I interrupted. "Why? I mean, how can this be? I can't believe it. I mean, I haven't done anything to them. I don't know of anything I could've…. It's all fucking crazy!" I exclaimed, "Sorry, Momma."

Then it hit me, and a shiver knifed through me unlike anything I've experienced before. I remembered the dream I had the other night. The dream I've had since I was a kid. It was too overwhelming to think that it might all be related to my soul and the events currently happening. *Was it really me? Was I involved in killing those people, or was it some part of me? And if so, does it actually relate to this series of strange events happening now?* The realization of this must have caused a strange look on my face.

"Are you alright, Mr. Drake?" O'Reilly asked.

"Uh, yeah. Yeah, I think so," I replied snapping out of the spell that had overcome me. "Momma, remember the dreams I had as a kid about killing Indians? Could those be related to this?"

"It isn't likely," replied O'Reilly, a look of dejection evident in his face and demeanor.

"It's *more* than likely," Swift answered quietly. "It's most likely that those dreams are part of your spirit carried through each generation as a dream, a memory, or it's actually your own memory carried in your soul from a past life experience.

"My people believe each life is but one chapter in the life of an endless spirit. This means that you would have been approached by these men whether or not you had stopped at Ten Mile Fork that day, and the fact that you have this medicine pouch is quite likely part of that warrior's plan. It may be easier for him to track you while it is in your possession."

"Boy howdy, that is some *wild* shit!" I exclaimed. Although it sounded about as far-fetched a story as one is ever likely to hear something deep inside me believed it. My fascination was followed by a deepening fear and then by a desperate desire to protect myself from these newly enlivened demons.

"So, if they are actually after me, how am I supposed to protect myself and my mother?" I fought off the butterflies in my stomach and sensed the heat rising in my blood.

"You're going to need to work with us, and I suggest you arm yourself. Reasoning with these warrior spirits will not be an option."

"Swift, advising civilians to arm themselves is foolhardy and not proper procedure," interjected O'Reilly. "Mrs. Drake, Mr. Drake, it might be more prudent if you were to get away for a little while until we've apprehended the men responsible. Please be aware that I have investigated many supposed 'paranormal events', and in nearly every instance we've solved the mystery behind the crime with a very mundane explanation.

"At this point I find it necessary to advise you that the Bureau has worked with Ben for over a year, but that the detective and I have only worked together for the past three months. I have as yet to verify any evidence of his story. We do have proof that people are killed or go missing and that much of the evidence is destroyed by fire wherever they go. We have no doubt we are dealing with sociopaths, and we've yet to find proof that it isn't they, themselves, committing these crimes. Let me repeat that it might be best if you were to get away until we are able to apprehend these individuals."

Swift showed no change in his demeanor as he listened to O'Reilly, and when the agent paused in his speech the detective turned back in my direction and spoke to me once again. "On the contrary, Mr. Drake, I highly recommend that you arm yourself, stay here, and help us locate these risen warriors, so we might gain proof of their existence and possibly put a stop to this. We have found nothing but death and destruction in their wake, and we've never had anyone survive their attacks but for you and your mother."

"Then how do you know what you're telling me is for real if you have never had a witness survive?" I asked a degree of doubt now creeping in supported by O'Reilly's rational explanation.

"Because..." Swift started haltingly. "Because I am a survivor. My forefather was a tribal policeman and was in attendance at the murder of Sitting Bull in 1890. I've had family die at the hands of these spirit warriors. Many other such killings were committed on the Pine Ridge and Standing Rock Reservations, and I saw six men performing this dance. A tribal elder, a man who actually knew the dancers, later told much of the story to me.

"For many years they confined themselves to killings of their own kind on the reservations and nearby towns, but they began branching out to other tribes, other parts of the country, some thirty years ago. A recent murder on the reservation reawakened my interest in these men, and I have tracked them ever since. When the FBI had a case that crossed paths with mine I agreed to work with them to find these men."

"And it is these same men," O'Reilly interjected, "that the Bureau and I believe are committing these killings. How they managed to appear to come out of whirlwinds, Mr. Drake, and how they completely destroy their victims are answers we'll get out of them once we've captured them. I think some of it is mere coincidence or some form of trickery they have managed to perfect. Frankly, this is the first time I've ever heard of them coming out of whirlwinds."

"Because you've never had a witness to talk to," Swift stated sharply.

"And how long has the FBI been pursuing these men?" Momma asked.

"Ma'am, the Bureau has been investigating these suspects for about a year. I'm the second agent to work with Swift. The first agent, Agent Flanders, began working with him about ten months ago, and now I am working with him."

"And the first agent?" I asked.

"Disappeared in a windstorm on the northern plains of Nebraska up along the Platte River the day after we reported there to investigate a case similar to the one you told us about at Ten Mile Fork." Swift looked straight at me as he answered.

"This gives me the chills," Momma said shakily.

It gave me the chills also, but I wasn't about to tell anyone. Though it reminded me that I needed to use the toilet real bad 'cause the thought of an armed FBI agent getting swallowed up made me feel a bit queasy. I remembered the dust twirling around my own feet at the Morales place. Knowing now that the bastard dust devils were purposely searching for me… Well, it gave me a real unsettled feeling.

"Excuse me a moment." Stepping out of the room, I headed into the bathroom to relieve myself. All the while I wondered how long I had before they got to me. Sweat broke out on my brow, and the clammy hand of fear wrapped its icy fingers around my soul. I trembled slightly as I fought off a bout of anxiety before gathering my wits and leaving the bathroom. When I returned to the front room the federal agent and the police detective were both on their feet.

"You boys leaving?"

"Yes, Mr. Drake. We best get back to our hotel. Would you and your mother mind accompanying us back to Lubbock?"

"And then what?"

"Well, we'll get written statements and follow any leads we might receive. You folks must have family nearby, people you can stay with?"

"I'd hate to drag family into this mess. Maybe we ought to just stay right here if ya'll don't mind."

"If you insist. The local police are keeping an eye on your place, and we can get official statements from you next time. Here's my card, and you be sure to contact us if these men show up again," O'Reilly stated handing me his business card.

"Mr. Drake, I'd like you to work with us on this if you don't mind," Swift stated. Even as the words flowed from his mouth his demeanor changed as though some new thought had struck a chord, and the words lost their meaning as they left his lips.

"I'm glad to work with ya'll, but I think I'm fixin' to be arrested. The county Sheriff and the Texas Highway Patrol are threatening to take me in. They think I'm the one committing these crimes."

"We'll talk with them," O'Reilly responded, "and see if we can get them to lay off for now. In the meantime you might want to reconsider my advice and get as far from here as you can."

"Actually, I'd like to stay here. I mean to find a place nearby." Swift spoke directly. "I need to see these killers for myself, and I can see nothing from my hotel room back in Lubbock. This is where they're going to strike. That warrior will return for this medicine bundle, but his primary target, I believe, is Mr. Drake. If we're going to catch these men it's necessary that we be where their potential victims are. I suggest we rent a camper or grab some gear and camp out right here."

"We can consider that," O'Reilly responded his eyes taking inventory of the simple house and tight quarters. "The Bureau has mobile units for such things, but in the meantime it's best that we return to Lubbock, review procedure, converse with the office in Washington, and consider our course of action."

"You're welcome to stay right here if you have a mind to, Mr. Swift." Momma stepped away from the wall, looking at the agents.

"You wouldn't mind if I stayed here with you?" Swift asked, looking at Momma and then looking at me.

"I'd prefer you did," Momma responded. "I would feel a whole lot safer."

"Well then, I'll remain here, and you can return to Lubbock and see if you can arrange some type of mobile unit." Ben Swift looked at O'Reilly. "Then we'll see if we can catch these *unwakanpi* in action."

It was obvious that O'Reilly didn't like it, but he was neither in charge of Swift nor did Swift's demeanor lend itself to argument. The two men stared at one another for a moment, but it seemed both of them recognized the other had his mind made up, and nothing was going to budge either of them.

"Suit yourself." O'Reilly turned to my mother, extended his hand, took hers into his own, and shook it genuinely. He thanked her for her hospitality and repeated his request that she contact him with any concerns or need for information. Then he turned to me.

"Mr. Drake, I can't stress enough the good sense behind my suggestion that you and your mother get away from here until we can catch these characters. It's bad enough they're running about killing people, but entertaining themselves by performing some sort of magic tricks during the commission of the crime proves they are very disturbed sociopaths at best. I fear that if you and your mother remain here it's quite likely that more harm will come to you.

"Unlike my associate here, I don't believe for a moment that some spirits are being conjured up whose sinister demons of the dust are looking for you directly. This being our first big break since the death of Agent Jack Flanders, the Bureau has decided to commit more manpower to the apprehension of these criminals, and several more agents are now en route to this location. If you and your mother could just get away, it's likely we'll catch them without any need for assistance. Now, Mr. Drake, you would like to assure your mother's safety, wouldn't you?"

Looking back at him I could see the sincerity in his eyes and heard it strongly in his words, but knowing that he didn't believe in these dust devils I felt no confidence in him. A week ago I'd have thought Detective Swift was a lunatic, but today it seems to me that he is as real as anything I know to be true, and I had to go with him on this one.

"I appreciate your concern, Agent O'Reilly, but I know what I've seen. Something in my heart tells me that these demons are after me and that no matter how far I run they'll follow me. So, I guess what I'm trying to say is that me and my mom are fixin' to stay right here until this is over."

Glancing quickly at Swift, O'Reilly grunted and headed for the door. "I'll brief the district office and let you know what they have to say.

Agent Winters and the rest of the team headed here from Washington should arrive soon. I suspect they may want to approach this a little differently."

With a quick nod, pausing briefly in the open doorway, O'Reilly went to his car. I got up and went to the door. Standing motionless I watched as he climbed into the sedan with government plates, and I was uncertain as to the sanity of my decision. I felt numb and turned back into the room only after the red tail lights of his car had disappeared from view.

❊ 7 ❊

Supper digesting nicely in our stomachs, Detective Swift and I settled comfortably in the lawn chairs beneath one of the desert willow trees in the backyard. We sat in silence as we watched the setting sun. Sipping from an ice-cold can of Coors I glanced at Swift. He released a plume of smoke from his lips and lowered the cigarette in his right hand before sipping beer from the can in his left. Then, setting the can down on an old wooden crate, he looked at me. "How are you holding up after all you've witnessed here of late?"

"Well, sir, I'm a bit freaked out. One of the damn things almost got a hold on me today. The damned whirlwind started twisting up around my feet, and it was a right eerie fucking feeling, I'll tell you that."

"Please, call me Ben."

"Okay, Ben. I didn't know what to do but to run when I first saw it. Today though, when I saw Scar Lip, that's what I call him because of the scar he has in his lip, I was angry that he'd messed with my Momma and killed Donny Jones. I have to admit I wanted to kill the son-of-a-bitch. I realize now that they can be hurt, killed probably, but at first I wasn't so sure. It's some freaky shit. I just wish they'd leave me alone."

"This Comanche had a deep scar in his lip?"

"Yeah. Why, does that mean something?"

Swift paused for a drag on his cigarette and sat silently for a moment before answering. "No. Like you, I need a way of identifying them. To reiterate what I told you earlier: they won't leave you alone, Brady. Especially now that you've caused them injury. They came here to avenge their own deaths and those of loved ones, and the way they were chosen means they died with vengeance in their souls. Despite

O'Reilly's belief that you could run it would serve little purpose other than delaying the inevitable. Unless we return these warriors to their graves neither you nor your mother will be safe."

"You seem to know a whole lot about these beings."

Ben looked away once again, turning his gaze toward the brilliant landscape illuminated by the sweeping colors of a sun surrendering to the advancing horizon. Drawing breath through his cigarette he exhaled wistfully as though considering his response carefully. As the bluish smoke rose into the warm evening air he shifted in his chair. "I feel a need to come clean with you, Brady, but what I tell you can go no further than you and me. What you hear must *never* be repeated."

His gaze held mine, and I realized he wouldn't say another word until I agreed. "You have my word."

Ben rose from his chair and walked to the center of the backyard. Inhaling smoke, he lifted his arms and blew it toward the sky. Turning to each of the four directions, he repeated this exercise and then stood in silent meditation before returning to his chair. Lighting a fresh cigarette he took a drag and looked me in the eye.

"Brady, I lied earlier today. But it's a lie I will tell again, for it is necessary for me to tell such a lie if I am to continue my work. I am not the descendent of a tribal policeman who was in attendance at the killing of Sitting Bull."

"You're not?" I asked, unsure how that was relevant.

Reaching for the can of beer he tipped it back for a long swallow. It seemed to me he was stalling as though what he would say came hard for him. Then, looking me square in the eye once more, he continued. "I *am* a tribal policeman who was in attendance at the killing of Sitting Bull."

For a moment there was only silence between us, and I peered back unsure if what he was saying was clear to me or if I had misunderstood him completely.

"Okay. What does that mean?" I stammered. "Didn't you say Sitting Bull was killed in 1890?"

"Yes. He was killed December 15, 1890. And I was there."

"So you're saying that you are over a hundred years old?"

"No, not exactly."

Pausing again to take a drag off the short nub of his cigarette before smothering it in the dust at his feet, Ben let me wait for an explanation. "Earlier I said that six dancers raise these warriors from the afterlife and return them to this one. Well, that's true. But at one time they were seven. I was the seventh one."

Again the detective paused while the astonishment on my face faded. *Is he one of them? Is he about to signal to the others to rush in from the neighbor's hedges while he rises up and shoots me dead?*

His gaze drifted to the horizon as though there, in the twilight, he might see the past unfold. "I was there when the soldiers of the Seventh Calvary, including a Sergeant Major Henry Drake, happened on a small band of people who were Ghost Dancing along Wounded Knee creek just before the massacre there that became so infamous. Six of us, tribal policemen, were accompanying the Army regulars and a rag-tag bunch of Home Guard on patrol when we happened on a dozen lodges in a coulee. Two-dozen men and women were dancing while several elderly folks and a couple of dozen children looked on.

"There was a strange aura about the place as we approached the circle of dancers. It felt downright eerie to me, and I know the others felt it as well. Not that they needed any reason to kill Indians, for they were prone to do so even in the most tranquil moments, but the others drew their weapons and talked nervously amongst themselves. The horses became skittish and had to be forced to continue toward the dancers. We were very close to the dancers when a young girl spotted us and shrieked. All hell broke loose. Some of the horses bolted, and others charged forward thinking they were going into action. The soldiers began firing immediately, and the dancers fell dead to the ground."

Pausing long enough to draw a swig from his can of beer, Ben shifted his gaze from the horizon to me for just a moment. I didn't move or even think of opening my mouth in response to what he had said so far. Looking once more into the fading sunlight he spoke with a wistful sadness that rattled something deep within me.

"I yelled for them to stop firing, but they had lost themselves in the act of killing, firing at the children and the elderly who had tended them. I could do nothing to stop it.

"It was then I spotted a group of boys huddled against an embankment standing waist deep in the icy water out of sight of the soldiers. Knowing the men would not stop until all were killed I spurred my horse toward the creek and positioned myself above the children, shielding their escape as they vanished into a thicket.

"Glancing in their direction I saw Dark Moon who nodded to me in thanks. I never thought I would see them again.

"Of the seven boys who managed to escape with my help one disappeared. I heard the others killed him, and six of them grew up together to become young men. All six began to practice the ghost dance, for they had seen a spirit stir that day on Wounded Knee Creek.

"I later learned they had seen snow whirling about on the land forming a whirlwind that is sometimes referred to as a snow-devil. When the soldiers entered the village the boys saw a young girl step from the snow-devil after it consumed the falling body of a small boy. In their senseless lust for killing the soldiers killed the girl immediately.

"Returning later the young boys gathered the ghost shirts, rattles, eagle bone whistles, drum, and the medicine bundles, things belonging to those who were engaged in the participation of that dance. They escaped to the sacred Paha Sapa, the Black Hills, and immediately began to emulate the dance in secret. Through the years, as they grew into men, they learned the secret. Eventually they perfected it.

"History knows it as the Ghost Dance. I call it the Shadow Dance because, although these dancers raise the spirits of the dead, they raise only spirits with a vengeful heart. These reanimated spirits are but shadows of who they once were. They have nothing but bloodlust and revenge in their hapless souls. They are incapable of love, of kindness, of forgiveness. They lack the feelings and essence that made our people great. They lack the fullness of spirit that made them the people they once were. They are but shadows of their original selves."

Again Ben paused, took one last drag from his cigarette before stomping it out underfoot, and finished off his can of beer. Reaching for another, he continued. "In 1903, while returning to the fort with a prisoner in tow, I was intercepted by Sheriff Hugh Bucknam and a posse of white men who were out hunting for my prisoner. Despite the sheriff's saying that he had jurisdiction and should take him in I denied them knowing Bobby White Bull wasn't likely to live long enough to stand trial if I didn't.

"I tried to skirt the posse with my prisoner in tow. When Sheriff Bucknam pulled his pistol the other men followed his lead, and I was gunned down along with the renegade. I remember the bastard sheriff plucking the badge from my coat. Then he said 'Ain't no Indian that don't need killing. The only good Indian is a dead Indian.' I died there on the snow-covered ground next to my dead prisoner.

"I suddenly found myself standing naked in the barnyard of a white farmer. Before me stood the farmer's wife, and she was shrieking. I guess the transformation of her husband into a naked savage was more than her heart could take, and she died of a heart attack right before my eyes. I wandered half a day before the boys found me. They wrapped me in a blanket, took me to their lodge and fed me, and then explained what had become of me.

"I ran with them for a lot of years. We wreaked havoc across most of the Dakotas and all along the Powder River basin. Sometimes we joined the raised warriors on killing sprees, and sometimes we just educated them to where they were and how they had come to be and set them loose. Some we never found, and they just picked up where they left off killing whites which was fine with us. A few became accustomed to their new lives, adjusted to living in the present time, and disappeared. But most of them simply killed until they died once again.

"And as for us, the Dancers, if one of us was killed the rest of us simply performed the dance. Only two drawbacks to this. The first is that the transformation is painful, disorienting, and can leave you vulnerable. And the second is you don't always come back with your mind fully intact. It's like you lose connection with a little bit of your soul each time you are returned. Like the spirit world keeps a little more for itself each time you transform. Fortunately for me, I seem to have few problems compared to what I've seen in others. Don't know why that is, but it is just that way."

"How many times have you come back? And why do you come back?" I asked.

Ben sat quietly for several moments, a practice I had now expected and become accustomed to.

"Well, Brady, the Dancers tend to insist on my return. I think Dark Moon would feel lost if he didn't have me on his tail. I am his nemesis, his Moriarity, you might say. He revels in defeating me, and in boasting how often he outwits me. He knows I will pursue him because it is only with his death, and the death of the Dancers, that my spirit will be set free.

"I died last year when Agent Flanders was killed. They brought me back. And that, Mr. Drake, is how I know O'Reilly doesn't know shit, but then he hasn't the capacity to recognize the truth. I am living proof."

My nerves were on edge. The story had me freaked *right* out, and it took me a minute to realize the man was finished. As I sat there, watching Detective Ben Swift light another cigarette, I still half-expected him to rise up, kill me, and call the rest of those demon bastards in from the shadows. But as he continued to smoke quietly, and sip his beer, I became calm. As the moments passed, questions replaced the fear that had gripped me only moments before.

"But, I've seen those demons and their eyes. Their pupils are enlarged, black as coal, and yours are normal, pretty much," I said, noticing the intense darkness of Detective Swift's eye color.

"The eyes return to being fairly normal once the desire for vengeance is released from the soul. Most of the Dancers have control over their hatred. The spirits they bring to life are chosen for their need for revenge, and most of them don't live long enough for their eyes to return to normal. My vengeance was satiated long ago. My only need now is to destroy the Dancers, so I can be free of this life."

In that moment I was intensely grateful to have an ally in my battle with the demons that I had no doubt might reappear at any moment. My mind was racing and Ben's story only generated new questions. "So, how did you…" I paused. "How did you end up being a police detective and chasing these dancers down?"

"In nineteen eighty-eight, we raised a batch of truly vengeful warriors. Unbeknownst to me they were men who I had killed when I was on the police force in the 1890s. When they rose up from the beyond, the first thing they did was kill three of my descendents: two women and a boy. The boy was a direct descendent of mine, through my son, Walks Proud.

"Anyway, I had watched my descendents from afar but befriended the boy and treated him like the great, great, grandson he was. When the warriors killed the boy and his family I killed the warriors, and the others didn't like it. Jacob Dark Moon and I had it out, and I left. I was sick of the killing. When they tried to kill me I fought them off, and when they set out on another journey of revenge I took out after them. But I lost their trail, and after a few months of trying to forget I found myself lying drunk in an alley. I went back to the only thing I knew and took a job as a Tribal policeman. I worked my way up to detective. And, as fate would have it, one of the first murder cases I received after getting my promotion turned out to lead me right back to Jacob and the rest of the bunch. I've been on their trail ever since. As for you, Brady Drake, you're nothing special. Just another descendent of an Indian killer. Truth be told, I knew Henry Drake. He was a Sergeant Major at the massacre I told you about. You look an awful lot like Henry. It's in your soul, and those bastards can smell it like a blood hound on a rabbit trail."

Thinking I needed another beer, I rose up and started toward the back door. "Another beer?" I asked Ben.

"No, I'm all set."

"Be right back." This was the wildest story I'd ever heard, and just knowing the blood-lusting killers were after me was disconcerting. My head filled with questions as I returned to the backyard. But, to my displeasure, Agent Swift had found my hammock slung between two cottonwood trees in the backyard, and a blanket. He was rolled up fast asleep. Returning to the house I called Rufus in for the night and retired to my bedroom. Every sound jacked my imagination and caused Rufus to growl and whine. It was another three hours before I finally dozed off to sleep.

❄ **8** ❄

September 1st

I awoke at my usual time: about 5:00 in the morning. Stumbling down the hallway, dressed only in my underwear, I stepped into the bathroom and performed the necessary tasks. After a quick shower I slipped into a clean pair of blue jeans and a white, sleeveless t-shirt.

I called out as I left the bedroom. Momma responded from the kitchen where she stood in her bathrobe waiting on the brewing coffee and watching Rufus who was inhaling a chunk of leftover meatloaf placed for him on the floor.

I leaned over and kissed Momma on the cheek before wandering to the back door to look out at Ben.

"Where did he go?" I mumbled as I stood stretching, staring at the empty hammock swinging in the breeze.

"He's around front and said for you to let him know when you were awake."

"Ugh." Returning to my bedroom I pulled on my cowboy boots and scooted back down the hallway through the living room to the front door. Pulling it open, squinting my eyes against the brilliance of the morning sun, I looked down at Ben as he sat on the edge of the porch with his back to the house.

"Good Morning, Ben."

"Same to you, Brady," he responded quietly as he got to his feet and stepped up onto the porch. In his left hand was a U.S. Geological survey map of the area. He'd obviously been working over it for some time because it was covered in red and yellow ink markings.

"What'cha got there?"

"Let's lay this out and maybe get a cup of that coffee I smell brewing."

Momma just happened to step onto the porch at that moment, with two cups of coffee in hand. "Detective. Brady," she said as she handed each of us a cup of steaming brew.

"Do you need cream or anything?" I asked Ben.

"No, black is just fine. Ah, Mrs. Drake?"

"Yes?" Momma turned back as she stepped through the door into the house.

"I was thinking on O'Reilly's suggestions as I sat here, and it might be a good idea if we could get you away from here for a few days. Would it be an imposition to ask you to move out until we have an opportunity to track down the Dancers?"

Momma stood for a moment looking from the detective to me and then back again. "Well, Detective, I suppose not if you think it would be safer. I hate to leave Brady."

"He'll be fine, ma'am. I have every intention of keeping him safe. He'll work with me over the next few days, and I promise to keep an eye on him the whole time."

"Brady, what do you think?"

"I reckon if Ben believes it is the best thing then maybe you ought to go on and listen to him," I answered, nodding as I looked over at her from my seat on the porch.

"But where would I go?"

"Do you have any relatives?"

"She has a sister nearby and a brother up north," I offered.

"My sister, Karen, lives over in Morton. I have a brother in Oklahoma City and a cousin in Denver, Colorado. I have a sister-in-law nearby, but I'd rather not impose on her." Momma's voice sounded tight and worried, and I couldn't help but think she was more worried about me than she was about imposing on her sister-in-law.

"Well, why don't we start by taking you to Morton. Hopefully that will prove to be far enough away from Brady. I'll ask O'Reilly to have Morton police keep a vigil on your sister's house. Does that sound okay with the both of you?"

My mother and I nodded our agreement.

"I'll pack a bag soon as we're done with breakfast," she murmured. Turning, Momma stepped back inside, and the screen door closed behind her. Ben sat down on the edge of the porch and spread his map out on the decking. I sat down opposite him, and focused on the indications he began making with his finger.

"I've pinpointed a few known battle sites of the Comanche from over a century ago on this map. To my way of thinking, the Dancers will most definitely gravitate toward some known or memorable place," Ben began, as I squatted down to gaze at the map. "We have little to go on as the Comanche were mostly unaffiliated bands who constantly roved about. They were nomadic peoples, like most of us on the plains and were tireless when it came to war.

"In addition to places where Comanche blood was spilled I've also been searching secluded locations central to where the recent strikes took place. That is, most likely, where we'll find the Dancers. They like to find a secluded spot where they can perform their rituals without risk of being detected. With the land so flat here and parcels so large they may just be set up in the middle of a field somewhere."

Momma returned with two plates of scrambled eggs, toast and bacon. Placing the plates on the deck between Ben and me she went back inside. Ben picked a piece of toast off one plate and took a bite while I picked up the other plate and began shoveling food into my mouth as fast as I could.

Continuing to study the map as I ate I was immediately intrigued by the lines of triangulation, marked in red ink, between the Morales place, Ten Mile Fork, and my house. Then it struck me: there was a large cavernous pit in the ground near the small town of Sundown that wasn't on the map.

"Right here," I pointed, "there's a hole in the ground. It's an old clay pit as big as a football field and, as you can see, in the middle of nowhere. We used to have bonfires and drinking parties there when I was back in high school. It's surrounded by fields of cotton and corn and would be a great place to hole up in."

Ben eyed the map, marking the spot I'd indicated with a pen.

"There's another spot right here." I pointed to another spot on the map. "It's an old, abandoned farm with a big tractor shed. That might be a good spot as well. And this area right here," I noted pointing again with my finger, "is a dried up oil lease, and it sits down in a little bit of a gully." I caught a piece of bacon as it fell from my open mouth before stuffing it back in and chewing happily.

Ben studied the map, marking the spots and jotting down notes while tracing the routes of nearby roadways. "Any other place that you think might accommodate our boys?"

"No, not that I can think of at the moment, but I reckon I'll come up with a few more if these don't pan out."

"Well then, why don't we get your mother to your aunt's house, and then you and I will check these places out. Give me a few minutes to wash up and we'll go," Ben said, standing up and folding his map before stepping inside the house.

"Okay." I finished off the food on my plate before taking up my coffee mug and washing down the last bit of toast. I set the plate down and turned my gaze toward the sun that continued to rise above the eastern horizon. A car passed by and I waved in response to a greeting from Mrs. Galveston, a local schoolteacher, who happened to be on her way to the school.

Staring out past the long abandoned Phillips 66 station across the street I let my eyes take in the grand view of the endless green fields of cotton extending all the way to the horizon. Sipping my coffee I pondered the strange turns my life had recently taken. While letting my legs kick back and forth as they dangled in front of the porch I realized that, for the first time since Ten Mile Fork, I was beginning to feel as though things could maybe return to normal at some point soon.

I had no sooner considered that possibility when I spotted something, or someone, moving across the fields a long way off. I thought at first it might be a farmer working his crops, or a deer, or maybe a horse that had wandered away from one of the local ranches. But no, whatever it was, it was running like a man, and then I spotted another and then another, and each one was moving steadily in my direction. The hair bristled on the back of my neck, and my gut tightened as I realized it was some of *them* running full bore across the field headed straight for town.

"Ben!" I called, my tone teetering on hysteria. Leaping to my feet and stepping directly into the plate containing Ben's breakfast, I suddenly wanted the only thing my Daddy ever gave me. Remembering that the few quality times we ever spent together were the times he taught me how to use it I was suddenly grateful to the bastard. What I wanted was my gun. In two steps, I crossed the porch and dashed into the house.

Ben and I collided as he came out of the bathroom and I squeezed around him on the way to my bedroom.

"They're comin'."

"They? You mean the warriors?"

"Yes," I replied as I leaped to my dresser and began tossing underwear and socks onto the floor as I looked for the metal box where I kept the Colt .45 revolver and several boxes of ammo. Pulling the encased weapon from the drawer, I wrestled the keys from my pocket. My fingers quivering and nerves on edge I unlocked the box. I loaded the weapon and leaped toward the closet where a well-oiled gun belt hung on a hook in the back.

Dragging it off the hook I cinched it on around my waist, spun the cylinders on the revolver to reassure myself that it was fully loaded, and slammed the weapon into the leather holster. I filled my hand with bullets and dropped them into my jeans pocket. Another handful of cartridges went into my other pocket as I lunged back into the hallway.

"Momma, get into the bathroom, lock that door, and don't come out until I come for you," I hollered as I turned and headed for the front door. Momma raced out of her bedroom half-dressed and her eyes staring up at me, wide with terror.

"They're coming, Brady?" she said tears welling up and her hands, clenching her blouse, rising to her chest.

"Yes, Momma, they're comin'. Now you get in that bathroom and lock the door."

She scurried across the front room and into the bathroom, locking herself in as I stepped out the front door. Ben Swift stood motionless in the shadows of the trees to the right of the yard, weapon in hand, a cigarette perched between two fingers on his free hand. His demeanor calm, he had strapped a second 9 mm Glock under his left arm. Stepping down from the porch I let my eyes scan the cotton fields across the street. I felt foolish when I saw nothing but green plants, stirred by a gentle morning breeze, waving in the fields across the road. "Did you see them? Where are they?"

Ben cocked his head sideways as though he were listening to something, something other than me. Pressing a finger to his lips, he signaled for me to be quiet and then motioned for me to walk over to where he was. "They're behind the house next door," he whispered just loud enough for me to hear as I stepped up next to him.

Drawing my weapon, I cocked the hammer and turned to look in the direction Ben had indicated. Dropping the cigarette at his feet Ben drew the second weapon, and instinctively we both squatted down weapons at the ready.

Seconds ticked by like hours as I strained to detect the demons. It occurred to me that they might have retreated and decided not to approach my home. But then I saw him, Claw Fingers, and he was creeping silently along the ground like a mountain lion preparing to pounce on unwary prey.

As though I had done it before, I rose up, aimed and fired—even as Ben's hand gripped my leg in an attempt to stop me. My bullet found its mark, blasting a hole through Claw Fingers' skull, and the demon slumped on the ground, his spirit returning to the hell from which I'm sure it came.

Oddly enough killing him felt good. It resonated with me in a way I never had known before, and gave me a momentary sense of *déjà vu*. I experienced a flash of boyhood memories and was reminded how bad I had felt when I killed a helpless armadillo. All I had done was raise that pistol and fire, without really aiming.

If I was nothing else I was a damned good shot. Even my Daddy had always bragged to his drinking buddies about how natural it was for me, as though I 'had done it in another life'. He'd been impressed by how quickly I took to it. My fondest memories of him are the memories of standing out in front of him and a couple of his drinking buddies, and firing at empty beer bottles while they drank and laughed. My Daddy loved to brag about my prowess with a handgun, a weapon three times the size of my small hands.

The shriek that followed broke me from my momentary revelry. Spinning to look behind me, I was stunned to see Ben grappling with Mohawk. Scar Lip and two other warriors bore down on us. Mohawk and Ben tumbled in the tall dried grass beneath the trees, battling for control of a gun gripped in Ben's hand and for a large knife in Mohawk's. Lunging for the second Glock that had fallen from Ben's other hand I turned my attention once again toward the charging warriors as one of them loosed a blood-curdling scream.

I raised my weapon and fired grazing Scar Lip's shoulder as he ducked. The gun in my other hand erupted, and the bullet passed through another demon's upper torso. Recoiling as the force spun him he tossed his shotgun to a gangly looking warrior to his right who whipped the shotgun upward and fired it prematurely. Molten buckshot ripped into my thigh as the majority of the lead balls slammed into the ground near me.

Skipping sideways and, wincing from the pain, I fired a rapid succession of shots at the oncoming trio, and they spread out to avoid the rain of bullets. Running toward Ben and the cover of the trees I dropped the empty Glock and shucked the empty castings from the six-shooter's cylinder and reloaded.

Mohawk, unable to get an upper hand, broke free of Ben's grasp. His eyes, now trained on me, noted my prepared weapon. Leaping backwards he spun away and vanished around the corner of the nearby house.

Pointing my weapon, I squeezed the trigger. The blast cut a hole through another demon as a group of them rushed to within five yards of where I pulled Ben to his feet with my free hand. Finding ourselves facing an onslaught of bullets Ben yanked me downward, and we bolted toward my house. A bullet grazed my neck and another cut a hole through my left boot as I fired a fatal shot into the forehead of the warrior I had just wounded. As we raced toward the house another blood-curdling war cry erupted somewhere to our front. Diving for cover near the porch we cowered as another barrage of gunfire erupted from the line of trees. Several arrows also whisked through the air, and some embedded in the porch floor. Laying low at the edge of the porch we exchanged gunfire with warriors in the tree line.

The hair rose on the back of my neck. Spinning around to look behind me I was shocked to find a long, silver blade slicing through the air towards Ben's back. Twisting in an awkward manner I fired, and the bullet shattered the half-naked warrior's knee. Collapsing on the wounded leg, the warrior fell on Ben and the razor-sharp implement only grazed the detective. As the warrior struggled to deliver a death strike Ben twisted and jammed his pistol up under the warrior's chin. Brains and blood erupted from the top of the demon-warrior's skull, and its body fell limp on the ground. In that same moment Rufus began to bark inside the house.

"Get to your mother!" Ben growled.

Fear for her gripped me as I charged along the north side of the house determined to reach the back door. Rounding the corner I was greeted by the sound of gunfire and the whine of bullets as they rocketed past my head. I struck the ground as I dove back in the direction I had come from. Bouncing to my feet I ran toward the front of the house. The fervor of Rufus's barking intensified, became a fearful yelp, then an eerie whining cry, and then stopped altogether. The ill feeling in my gut assured me that someone other than my mother was inside the house.

Leaping onto the front porch, ignoring the bullets whizzing around me, I watched in amazement as three more Comanche warriors sprinted out of the cotton fields across the street and raced toward me. The maniacs were armed but struck everything and anything but their intended targets. I fired a defensive volley of shots and dashed across the porch with Ben hard on my heels.

Our bodies slammed in unison against the front door. It gave way, and we fell through the opening sprawling across the floor in my living room. A hailstorm of bullets and arrows kicked up dirt, struck the porch, and peppered the front wall as we scrambled to our feet and searched for any assailants inside the house.

"Check the back door," Ben hissed, his eyes watching the front yard as he kicked the front door shut.

My anxiety deepened when I realized the door to the bathroom had been kicked in, shattered beyond repair. A quick look inside fueled my fear as I ran to the kitchen. The back door was completely ripped away. Then I spotted Rufus. The poor dog lay in a spreading pool of his own blood with his head nearly severed from his body.

"Momma!" I shrieked as I tore across the kitchen and peered outside. "Momma!" I shouted again and ducked as a volley of rifle fire let loose from beyond the trees—every round focused on the back door to the house. Returning fire, I reloaded my weapon, squatted low, and dashed out into the sunlight. Firing as I ran, I desperately searched for any sign of my mother as I dove once more for cover.

The distant wail of a siren approaching Broken Spoke interrupted the terrifying thoughts filling my head. Noting that no one was shooting at me I left the cover of the tool shed and ran toward the front of the house.

"Ben! Ben, they've got her," I shouted, running up onto the porch.

Just then a police cruiser raced into my front yard. Skidding across my front lawn, raising a cloud of dust, it came to a halt. Guns in hand, officers lunged out of both front doors before aiming their weapons directly at me. The wailing siren of another police cruiser indicated reinforcements were on the way. Leaping off the porch, I took several steps in their direction, with the intent of gaining their assistance.

"Put the gun down!"

"Drop the weapon!" commanded a second officer.

"They've taken my mother!" I yelled, hesitant to relinquish my weapon.

"Toss the weapon aside, and lie down on the ground."

"Just do it, Brady," barked the familiar voice of Ben Swift still sheltered inside the house.

Reluctantly, I tossed the handgun to my left and lay down on my stomach as the policeman approached me all the while scanning the area for any sign of the ruthless bastards who had filled my front yard only moments before. As an officer knelt on my back and looped handcuffs around my wrists I realized that not only had the arrows vanished, but also the bodies of the warriors I had killed.

"You there, inside the house, come out with your hands in the air," bellowed one officer, his weapon now trained on the front door. The other officer, completing the task of handcuffing me, stood and yanked me to my feet.

"Take it easy," I growled.

Bumping me intentionally as he passed, the officer stepped around in front of me and leaned close to my face as though he intended to address my complaint. Just then, the front door of my house snapped fully open and Swift called out.

"I'm a police officer, and I'm coming out," he called, his weapon visible and snugly secured inside his shoulder harness. Ben held one hand high in the air while the other gripped his wallet-shrouded badge extended before him.

Another police cruiser charged into the yard, and two additional Levelland police officers leaped out immediately joining the others with their weapons aimed at Ben. Each of them watched intensely as the man walked from the house and crossed the yard. He surrendered with both hands in the air. Another siren could be heard wailing in the distance.

Stepping up to Ben, one policeman grabbed the badge while another kept his weapon trained on the detective. "Is this real?" the officer asked as he looked at the tribal policeman's badge.

"Yes, of course it's real."

"Well, whether it is or isn't, you've got no jurisdiction here. This here says you're from South Dakota; someplace called Pine Ridge to be exact. What the hell are you doing here in Texas?"

A second officer reached forward and yanked the Glock out of Ben's shoulder harness and backed off several steps, keeping his gun pointed at the detective. "Where's the other gun?" the second officer asked, nodding at Ben's other armpit.

"I'm working with the FBI on a case here, and this man is working with us. I can give you the phone number to the agent I'm assisting. If you'll take a minute to call him he can verify it. The other weapon is hereabouts somewhere."

"This man is Brady Drake," barked the officer holding me by the handcuffs and looking up from my wallet, "and he's currently a suspect in a series of murders, arson cases, and missing person incidents."

"Well, your superiors will be notifying you that this man is working with Federal agents and me in an attempt to track down those responsible for your missing and murdered. I will gladly give you Agent Wilson O'Reilly's phone number, so you officers can give him a call and verify my story."

"That won't be necessary." I looked up to see Sheriff Hugh Baker climbing out of his cruiser as he continued to speak. "We've already been notified of your presence, Swift, and of your apparent affiliation with the FBI. You boys can let this man be, and take the cuffs off Mr. Drake. Much as I'd personally prefer you didn't."

Responding to the stern look from Sheriff Baker the patrolmen released me while another returned Ben's weapon as well as my own. Taking away his handcuffs, the deputy slapped my chest with my wallet and released it. I caught it and stowed both the wallet and weapon in their rightful places.

"What, in God's name, or more'n likely the Devil's, have ya'll been up to here?" Sheriff Baker asked. "We've had reports of shots fired and half-naked men running in the streets."

"My mother…" I shut my mouth when I received a glare from Ben.

"Yes, your mother?" Sheriff Baker lowered his brows and his eyes narrowed slightly.

"His mother is with relatives. As to the situation here, we were attacked by a couple of suspicious looking men who resisted my inquiry as to the reason for their lurking about. Shots were exchanged and they ran off." Swift intervened with an explanation.

"Is that so?" Baker responded.

"Yeah, that's what happened." The words burst out, lacking conviction, as I reflected on what had actually happened all the while wanting desperately to ask these officers to begin a search for my mother.

"If your mother is with relatives why did you just mention her, Mr. Drake?"

"Ah, well, I knew you met her before, and I just wanted you to know she wasn't here."

"Uh-huh," he said, doubt evident in his tone. "Well, I'm sure whatever is going on here my men and I will likely have to clean up one heck of a mess once you and the FBI get done screwing things up." Baker looked at Swift. "And I do sincerely hope that no more of our citizens suffer during that time.

"As to you, Mr. Drake, you may have these bigwigs kowtowed into believing you ain't responsible for what has gone on. But, as for me, I ain't buying any of it. I know at some point you'll step on your own dick. And when you do rest assured I'll be right there to stomp on you and see to it you swing at the end of a noose for it."

"They don't hang people anymore, Sheriff." I looked back at him my gaze level and defiant.

"I'll see to it that they make a blessed exception in your case," Sheriff Baker growled, a scowl forming on his face as he leaned in my direction.

I stood silent, looking at my own reflection in his chrome-tinted sunglasses and wondering where my mother was and if she was still alive.

"We've things to do, if you don't mind, Sheriff," Swift said.

"Sure thing, detective. I was just fixin' to say the same thing. You boys go on and play, and we'll keep an eye out for ya'll," Baker answered smugly. "And Drake... You just reached the top of my shit list, and these Feds won't be around forever." Baker turned and walked back toward his cruiser his eyes combing the area as he did so.

Ignoring him, I turned away and approached Ben as the other lawmen crawled into their cruisers and pulled away. Swift motioned with a nod of his head for me to follow and, after he had retrieved his second weapon, we continued toward the back of the house.

"Why didn't you let me report my mother's kidnapping?"

Ben indicated a request for my silence and the severity of his action induced me to postpone my questioning. Following Ben, the two of us walked into the backyard. Bending on one knee, the detective studied the ground just outside the backdoor. Silently, he stood and crossed through the trees into the neighbors' yard. I followed him through several back yards and then out onto the street.

"It appears our attackers returned to the cotton fields with your mother in tow. We'd best begin searching for the Dancers. Where they are these warriors and your mother are likely to be." Ben spun on his heels and began walking back toward my house.

"How do you know she's not laying dead out there in the fields somewhere? And why didn't you let me get the cops to help us find my mother and get her back?"

"If we had told the Sheriff that Claudia had been abducted we would be filling out reports right now. That wastes valuable time. And if we start a major manhunt and the Dancers catch wind of it they'll skedaddle for sure. Then it could be months or years before I get another chance to get this close to them. As to your mother… If they wanted to kill her they would have done it here. They took her, which means they will return with her to the Dancers. Why they didn't just kill her is a bit of a mystery, but I'm guessing they want to draw us out. The only other reason is they wish to barter for something. Maybe you have something belonging to the Comanche or there is something the Dancers want from you. Do you have anything other than the medicine pouch?"

I thought for a moment before I answered. "No, we've nothing that belongs to anybody."

"Well," Ben said, detaching the phone from the clip on his belt as we stood in front of my bullet-riddled and damaged home, "I'll brief O'Reilly as to our intentions, and we best begin searching for the Dancers and your mother."

With the phone to his ear, Ben slipped back inside the house to retrieve his map. Minutes later, after we had attended to my wounded leg, seated in my pickup truck, we headed south out of town. The damage to my house, and mess inside, would have to wait.

$$\text{※ } 9 \text{ ※}$$

"This road has definitely been traveled recently," I said, confirming Swift's observations of fresh tire tracks in the earth. The crop fields running along either side of the dirt road approaching the old Altman house had been recently plowed, but fields were always in some state of use by someone whether the houses they surrounded were inhabited or not.

"These old farmhouses often have migrant workers livin' in them," I told Ben, "but they're just as likely to sit vacant for long periods of time in between crop hands." Close up, it was apparent that this particular house had sat one too many years beneath the hot Texas sun and was pretty well done for. Some of its windows were broken out, the front door was gone, and the porch roof had fallen in a while back. Its wooden frame was dried to tinder, and the gray clapboards had long ago shed their paint. From the looks of it, it wasn't likely to ever see another human living beneath its hole-ridden roof.

Apart from the creak and hum of a nearby pump jack, nothing but the rustling of dried leaves in a nearby cottonwood disturbed the eerie silence of the long-abandoned farm. Seated in the parked truck we were surrounded by the endless plains of northwest Texas.

We stepped out of the vehicle and looked about the place. The only evidence of anyone having been there recently were cases of empty beer bottles strewn about the shed. Finding nothing to lead us to believe that the Dancers or their spawn had visited the place we decided to move on to the next spot I had pointed out on the map.

It took us a half hour to drive to the old clay pit southeast of the Altman place. Ben tensed up when he noticed some movement in the brush next to the road just at the point where the road began its descent to the bottom, but nothing more than a jackrabbit leaped from the sun-dried thicket. It seemed to me that Ben had become a bit nervous, as though he sensed something, but he said nothing about it as we drove down into the pit and turned the vehicle around. Moments later, we were again approaching the paved road.

"More secluded spots hereabouts than I suspected." Ben broke the silence as we hit the asphalt.

"Ya reckon?" I replied. "Seems to be the more I think on it the more pits and abandoned farms I recollect. Let me see the map, and I'll point them out for you." Stopping in the middle of the road, I leaned over the unfolded chart and scanned it quickly.

"I think they may have visited that last pit, though I can't say for sure. Just a hunch, but I bet we'll find them in something like it when we finally come up on them," Ben mused.

"Well, there are holes like that all over west Texas, and several holes like that around here," I said, tapping with my finger.

As Ben leaned over the map I pointed out some other plausible hiding places. Three of the spots were just outside Ben's triangle while a few others were located within its confines. We spent the next four hours having a look around several pits and places I considered off the beaten path. We found little of interest, although at a sharecroppers shack near Lehman we found what Ben called Peyote buttons which he said might have belonged to one of Dancers we were after. We couldn't be sure, though. He said the new Comanche church also used them for religious purposes.

We swept along a dozen back roads looking for signs wherever I thought it possible for an encampment to be located. As we drove along in the heat of an aging Texas afternoon a thought crossed my mind. "Ben, how is it that these spirits rising up are all bloodthirsty and vengeful, as you said, and not pleasant folk?"

The detective said nothing for a long time, and I was beginning to think he wasn't going to answer me at all when he finally spoke. "Spirits tend to respond to like energy. The Dancers, and the bastards they spawn, are of a vengeful spirit and vibrate at that frequency. If you think about tuning in your radio it's rare that a country station comes in over a rock station frequency even though it does happen if conditions are just right. On occasion someone other than an angry, vengeful soul emerges, but rarely."

"So these things ain't always bloodthirsty demons?"

"Seen a young girl up in Nebraska one time. She was found naked sitting alongside the highway next to the backpack belonging to a hitchhiker in his forties. His wallet and I.D. were inside, but he was never seen again. Authorities had her institutionalized when she didn't respond to their line of questioning. Social worker from the Reservation spoke to her in Lakota. She told her she was Hunkpapa and remembered dying from smallpox in her tepee. I knew the Dancers were connected."

"What happened to her?"

"Still there as far as I know. She must be near forty years old now. Heard she'd been declared insane."

Ben paused, lit a cigarette and blew several smoke rings. "They raised another man one time. He had been a peaceful man, a healer, and went crazy from the shock of this time and place. He wandered a bit, drunk and homeless, before they found him dead in an alley down in Omaha."

"I reckon it would be an awful shock to suddenly awaken in another time."

Ben went quiet then and simply rode along in silence smoking his cigarette. "There's a lot of good people could be raised, people who could lead our people back to the greatness that was once our pride. But Dark Moon isn't interested in the souls of the good. He seeks only the vengeful. Seems an awful waste of a mighty power."

He didn't speak again until we got back to the Altman place an hour later and pulled onto the main road. Even then it was just to ask me to pull over so he could take a leak.

Suddenly I remembered a second quarry situated nearby. Crossing the paved highway we rolled along another dirt road, passing several cattle guards before pulling into a narrow path. It turned out to be another dead end.

We spent the rest of the day traveling back roads and cow paths but found no trace of the Dancers. As the sun sank toward the horizon I grew weary of searching, and I suggested to Ben that we ought to contact the authorities and get more people searching for Momma.

"I understand your anxiety, Brady, but this is big country and even with the few more men they might provide it could prove to be very difficult. Especially since the Dancers aren't likely to remain in one place too long. I have a feeling that we will find them near a place of death, a place where a great battle took place. These places, places where spirits left the bodies, are the best locations to incite and inspire the energy of the ghostly specters to return."

"Well then, how are we going to find such places?"

Ben sat quietly for several minutes and stared off across the prairie. "I know of a Comanche who was raised, a man named Isatai, and I believe he lives up near Amarillo. He returned from the dead about near fifty years ago when Dark Moon and the rest of us made a little foray down this way. We didn't stay long that time, but long enough to rise up a few Comanche. Isatai was one of them. He was a fearsome warrior and raged across these southern plains for near ten years before something happened, and he lost his desire for vengeance.

"Jacob seeks guidance from locals whenever he enters an area. He has been to Texas a few times since that first jaunt fifty years ago, and Isatai has been his resource down here each time. Last I heard of Isatai he had a small spread up Amarillo way with a few head of cattle. I think it would be wise for us to go have a talk with him and see if he can be of any help to us."

"Don't you think we just ought to keep looking, Ben? I can't stand the thought of Momma being out there somewhere overnight. God knows what they might do to her."

"Think about it Brady; we're talking hundreds of square miles. We could search for days and still not find her. I suspect Isatai knows where they might be. He was a powerful warrior and holy man in his day, and I suspect he can pinpoint a few spots where they might be. It'll be dark soon making it more difficult to search for Claudia and her captors. But we can get up to Amarillo and back overnight and start fresh in the morning."

Silence filled the cab and remained until I pulled the truck out onto the main road. I felt that Ben was waiting for me to agree, but it took me a while before I could see the logic in his argument. I didn't have any faith in this Isatai character but Ben did, and I believed Ben was sincere in his belief.

"All right then, let's get on up near Amarillo."

Ben nodded, and I turned the truck east. While the road passed beneath the spinning tires my mind spun with images of my recent past and imaginings of my immediate future. I began to calm about the time we reached Route 87, just south of Lubbock, and turned north.

The late day sun gave way to twilight which soon succumbed to darkness as we headed toward Amarillo. Few words passed between us as we journeyed through the darkness. The lights of Amarillo had faded behind us for some time before Ben instructed me to leave the highway. We traversed miles of back road while Ben talked to several people on his cell phone—sometimes in a language I didn't understand—while attempting to locate the whereabouts of this man Isatai.

It was late when I noticed we were low on fuel, and we had to make our way back to the main road to find a gas station. It was no small feat finding one open at this time of night, but we managed. Returning to the pitch black of the countryside, Ben guided us for another forty minutes navigating miles of narrow dirt roads. After a while he grunted and pointed a finger at the illuminated windows of a small ranch house set back a hundred yards from the rugged and desolate road on which we traveled.

❈ **10** ❈

Pulling into the driveway, we approached the house. It was a small, squat ranch house with an empty corral, a barn, and a creaking windmill. An old pickup truck with more primer than paint sat near the fence not far from a tractor that was in similar condition. When I was within twenty yards of the dwelling two German shepherds approached us from the shadows, their eyes wide and ears pinned back. They began to growl and whine as I slowed the truck to a halt. Suddenly a large man appeared as though he manifested from the shadows near the house and had not been there before. He approached the vehicle shotgun in hand.

Heat lightning flashed in the distance, and the low rumble of thunder cast a spell of foreboding across the land. Ben lowered the window as the man stepped up to the truck.

"I'm looking for Isatai," Ben said quietly.

The large man, massive in breadth and fullness of muscle, dressed in blue jeans, a western style shirt, and wearing a ball cap stared at each of us for a long time before answering. "And who are you?"

"Ben Swift, a police officer from Pine Ridge, South Dakota. And this here is Brady Drake, a man from down near Levelland. We mean no harm. We just have a few questions we'd like to ask."

"You both armed?"

"Yes."

"Wait here."

The man turned away and strode toward the house. The two German Shepherds continued staring at Ben from only a few feet away. The door on the house opened just long enough for the man to pass through, then closed swiftly behind him.

Ben and I said nothing as the minutes ticked by. It seemed as though an eternity passed before the large man made his way back to my truck. He sauntered up to Ben's window and spoke in a hushed voice. "Come. But your friend must stay in the truck."

"Okay."

Ben glanced at me, nodded in reassurance, and stepped out of the vehicle. The dogs released a guttural growl but remained where they were with their eyes now fixed on me. The two men made their way to the house and disappeared inside. My eyes roamed the darkened landscape. At random, lights twinkled in the distance, and thousands of stars gleamed clearly in the night sky. Despite the heat a breeze blew gently across the darkened land. For half an hour I sat in silence, glancing at the clock on the dash from time to time, and wondered if all was well within the house. Just as my concern began to inspire thoughts of possible action the front door swung open, and Ben and his escort returned to the truck.

"Thank you, Nara," Ben said, climbing into the cab. "Let's go." Ben shut the door behind him. I started the truck and backed up before cutting the wheel and heading back along the narrow trace toward the road.

"Any luck?"

"No, but Jacob was here. He and his troupe camped here about a week ago. I think Isatai could truly be of help to us, but it seems he hopes to remain in Jacob's good graces. Isatai is quite old now, and he wants the Dancers to bring him back when he dies. But he says Jacob refused his request to be raised again because he no longer seeks revenge against his former enemies. Because he hopes Jacob will reconsider he won't help us. It is unfortunate for us that he doesn't know Jacob. Jacob's only loyalty is to himself."

We had only gone a short distance when I felt the need to look up. My blood ran cold. Flaming arrows descended on the small house in my rearview mirror, and several half-naked warriors leaped from the darkness beyond the horse stable. A dozen more rose up from the ground on either side of my truck. Ahead of us, I could see more of them running down the dirt trace in our direction. Seeing the flickering light of the flames, which quickly spread across the house, Ben turned and looked back.

"Back up, Brady. Head for the windmill beside the corral."

My heart raced and I felt a surge of panic flood my veins. Slamming the truck into reverse, I gunned the engine, and we sped backward. I hit the brakes just before slamming into the rail fence, stopping only a few feet from where Nara stood. The man gave us a hard look before spinning around, lifting his shotgun as he did so. Killing the first three men charging him, Nara worked quickly to reload. With a nearly silent command he set his dogs on the furthest combatants. Ben's hands were immediately filled with the twin Glocks he yanked from the double shoulder harness. He fired at the warriors approaching Nara protecting the man as he fed fresh shells into the twelve-gage shotgun.

I'm not sure if it was a sound or just instinct that caused me to turn and look out the window on my side of the truck as I was pulling my pistol, but I barely ducked in time to miss the long bladed knife that would have been embedded in my skull. Having leaned toward Ben, I raised the gun and fired, blasting a hole in the forehead of my attacker. The anxiety I had been feeling only seconds before transformed into an adrenaline powered need to kill.

Straightening, I fired at four more warriors, killing three and sending a fourth scampering away toward the cornfield bleeding from his lower back. Armed with knives, most of the warriors didn't stand a chance of reaching us. Suddenly, a burst of gunfire erupted from the cornfield. I heard the back window of the cab shatter, and I knew immediately that I was hit as a searing burning sensation ripped across my shoulder.

Shoving up against me, Ben pointed both his weapons toward the muzzle flash amongst the tall, leafy stalks and fired until both his weapons were empty.

"Get out," he shouted, pushing me as he yanked on the door handle. Grabbing the Remington Carbine from the window rack, I cursed as Ben and I both tumbled out of the truck. Rolling across the dirt, I sat up and pointed my pistol toward the cornfield as a second round of firing erupted. Ben ran to my left, maneuvering toward the house. I snatched up my rifle and followed him.

Swept by the wind, flames covered the roof and engulfed the east end of the structure. Smoke poured from a front window where the glass had been shot out.

Nara and Ben hit the front door at about the same time, and both men disappeared inside. Diving for cover behind an antique tractor parked near the western corner of the house I fired on the numerous warriors charging the burning abode.

Ben and Nara reappeared, leaping out of the decaying shanty with a feeble old man strung between them. Staggering from the smoke filled dwelling the men coughed as they moved in my direction. Isatai was dressed in overalls, cowboy boots, and a calico shirt. His long, silver braids hung down across his shoulders. Despite his aged body and cracked skin his eyes gleamed with the same silver brightness as his hair. Providing cover fire for the three I holstered my empty Colt and resumed firing with my fully loaded Remington.

Gunfire erupted once again from the cornfield. Bullets raked the house, tractor, and the old Chevy pickup truck parked only a few feet from where we all huddled for cover. Nara was struck as he squatted down to set Isatai behind the tractor. Blood spurted from his hip as he grunted and pivoted from the impact of the shot. Freeing himself from Isatai, Ben lurched upward and began firing both handguns in the direction of the attackers.

Out of the corner of my eye I saw two men skirt around the end of the house with guns in hand. I turned my weapon on them and began firing but not before they let off several shots of their own. Isatai was hit twice while a third bullet took the hat off Nara's head. Nara returned fire with an eerie calm, killing one of the warriors while I gunned down the other.

"Get to the stable!" Ben shouted.

Grabbing up a severely wounded Isatai, Ben and a limping Nara made for the stable. The three-sided barn was constructed with chest high corral partitions made of wood and a waist-high front wall constructed of mud brick. Dashing past the rail fence the four of us took cover by squatting down behind the front wall. Bullets raked the structure causing some of the wooden boards above us to splinter.

Reloading my weapons, I peered out through a gap in the mud-brick. A dozen Comanche warriors were now creeping toward our location. The *thud, thud, thud* on the roof followed by a brightening of the night told us all that firebrands had been unleashed, and our meager shelter would not provide us protection for long. Erupting from the guns of the approaching warriors, bullets again sprayed the entire stable. Isatai was hit in the belly, Nara and Ben suffered flesh wounds, and I was grazed on my left forearm. We attempted to return fire, but every time we stuck our heads out we were met with a barrage of hot lead. I thought of Momma and J.J. and Billy Don, knowing they would miss me the most, because it seemed to me I was going to die right there in that burning stable.

But it was in that instant of realization that, I reckon, a small miracle occurred. I can only speculate what caused the leak of natural gas, but the full front of the small house suddenly exploded, killing most of the warriors charging down on us and sending several more running wildly about with flames covering their bodies. We dispensed of the flaming bastards with ease since they were a little more distracted with burning to death.

"We've gotta get out of here," Ben commanded. "Let's get to the truck."

With the house and the stable completely engulfed in flames the area was brightly lit, and as we crept toward the vehicles we saw no other combatants. Looking on Isatai, I could tell that he had been mortally wounded. He bled from his neck and on the left side of his torso from both the chest and abdomen. Nara had been hit in the left thigh, and his hip still bled. Ben had taken a bullet in the leg also. I quickly tore away my shirt and cinched a makeshift bandage around Ben's leg and Nara's shortly after. Suddenly Isatai, who lay on the ground between the two men, coughed up blood.

"Let's get Isatai up into the truck," Ben urged Nara.

Isatai pulled on the two men and spoke in a language I didn't understand. Nara bent low to the man's face and listened intently, sadness visible on his bloody, soot-stained features. Isatai spoke until the blood and coughing made speaking impossible. His eyes opened wide as he writhed violently in spasm, and then his body went limp. The old Indian's head fell back on the earth, and his eyelids lay back. Isatai's vacant stare peered out beyond the sparks and flames to the darkened heavens above.

Nara whispered a subdued song of prayer and reached down to close the man's sightless eyes. After a few verses his gaze turned toward Ben.

"Isatai said the men you seek will be found in a deep depression somewhere near Canyon Del Rescate. He said a major battle took place there between our people and the Bluecoats. Says women and children were slaughtered trying to escape when the warrior and Comanchero positions were overrun. Says much Comanche blood was spilled in that place. He says Dark Moon asked him for such a place, and that is where he directed him to go. He wants you to know this."

"Brady and I have to go there as quickly as possible."

"I'll go with you, but I have to bury him first." Nara nodded toward Isatai.

"We'll help you."

"We must bury him according to ancient tradition the way his last body was buried."

Ben nodded in agreement and looked at me. "Brady, you stand guard. I think they may have retreated, but we don't know if they'll stay gone."

"Okay," I replied, feeling a wave of anxiety begin to creep over me. I just wanted to go. I didn't really care about burying this old Indian; I just wanted to get to my mother. And I didn't believe for a second that the others had retreated. As I backed up against the antique Chevy truck and began to look around the two men set to performing the burial rite with Nara providing instruction.

Nervously, I kept turning about, watching for any sign of other Comanche warriors, but I'll admit that I was somewhat distracted by what the other two men were doing and glanced at them when I dared.

Ben peeled a length of rope from a nearby corral post while Nara went to the old truck and withdrew a beaded leather satchel that had been hanging on the mirror. Kneeling above the lifeless corpse he produced a paintbrush and bottle of paint. While Ben pulled the knees up and folded Isatai's thighs against his abdomen, Nara painted the dead man's face a bright red. Ben slid the rope under Isatai's buttocks and cinched the man's legs in place leaving him with his knees tied securely to his chest. Nara then packed large daubs of clay over Isatai's eye sockets. This done, Nara limped toward the stable and retrieved a shovel.

It was at that moment that a howling warrior burst from the mesquite trees beyond the stable and bore down on Nara with a large knife in hand. Lifting my rifle I shot the vengeful bastard dropping him with a hole in the center of his skull.

My nerves once more on edge I continued to move. I paced warily, constantly turning, watching the shadows in all directions.

Nara set to the task of digging a hole near the corral fence, and when it was nearly three feet deep he stepped up out of it and made his way to the Chevy pickup truck, wrestling a blanket from behind the seat. He walked to where Isatai lay on his side in a fetal position before standing silently looking down at the body and mumbling something. The man then knelt and wrapped Isatai in the blanket. Picking up the old man's body, Nara returned to the hole and sat the corpse upright in the bottom of it. He then shoveled the dirt into the grave while quietly singing a song in his native tongue. When all but the top of the skull had been covered with the red dirt of northern Texas, Nara pointed to a small pile of stones. He and Ben made several trips until they had transferred the rocks from there to the top of Isatai's grave. This done, Nara retrieved his shotgun and the ornamental satchel. He then looked first at me and then at Ben.

"If we leave now we can be in position to attack by sunrise."

"You're sure you want to go with us?" I shook my head, my eyes on Nara's hip where he'd been shot.

"I've no need to stay here. I cared for Isatai in his frail condition, and now he has crossed over. I will avenge his death."

"Good. Another gun won't hurt," Ben said, and the three of us walked toward my truck. Nara was in the lead when a hailstorm of gunfire erupted once more from the cover of the cornstalks east of the house. Bullets struck Nara with such force that he staggered backward before jerking sideways, slamming into the tailgate on the rear of my truck, and falling to the earth.

Ben and I dropped to the ground and returned fire. Crawling in the dirt we sought cover as the bullets plowed the earth around us. Reloading several times, we managed to drive back the attackers concealed in the cornfield. Then we crawled forward and continued to fire so we could pull Nara to the relative safety beside the truck.

Ben's cursing was the first indication I had that Nara died from the newly inflicted wounds. We had no time to consider his death because the gunfire started once more. The source of the fire was centered at the far end of the skeletal remains of the smoldering house.

"We're going to end up like him if we stay here. We'll lay some heavy fire into that cornfield and try to flank them. Follow my lead," Ben growled at me.

Leaping to our feet we fired as we ran. We crossed the open ground at full tilt and entered the tall corn and began cutting across the field in an attempt to get behind the riflemen.

Despite the adrenaline running through my veins I suffered a moment of anxiety just as we stumbled on them. Two men, squatting down and running in our direction, slammed into us in the darkened maze. All of us fired at once and I heard one man cry out as I staggered backward with my own weapon blazing. A streak of heat rushed through my side as I tripped and fell backward. Striking the ground, I lay still until the gunfire ceased and silence filled the air.

"Ben," I hissed.

A muzzle flashed just to my right followed by the rapid pounding of Ben's Glocks, his weapons unleashing a barrage of heated lead. The warrior fell heavily onto the dirt, striking the ground only a few feet from where I lay.

"Brady?"

"Yeah, yeah, Ben, I'm right here."

"You hit?"

"Yeah, but I think I'm fixin' to be all right. You?"

Ben appeared squatting next to me and helped me to my feet. "Let's get back to the truck."

Inching our way through the darkness we emerged from the cornfield. Then, while walking across the open ground toward the truck, I spotted the corpses of Nara's dogs. I remembered seeing them several times during the fight, engaged in battling the warriors. Their once menacing forms now lay docile, lifeless in the dirt, their fur encrusted with their own blood. For a moment I felt a bond with these two creatures. We hadn't been friends, but we had battled against a common enemy.

Retrieving the first aid kit from behind the seat of my truck, Ben and I took turns patching one another up. He was quite adept at sewing stitches to close the gash in my side and the hole in my shoulder. I winced a bit and tried to appear unaffected by the pain it caused.

"We better give Nara the same treatment we gave Isatai," Ben said quietly as I stowed the medical kit behind the seat.

"Do we really have time?" I asked, thinking about my poor mother.

"We will make time."

"All right."

"Check the truck and around the stable for a blanket and some rope."

It took me a good ten minutes to locate a blanket and a length of rope. Ben had applied the paint and clay to Nara's face by the time I returned to the body. In silence we tied the legs in place and wrapped the large man in the blanket. Grabbing the shovel I dug a hole, grimacing for each grain removed. It wasn't long before we had the body seated snugly in its grave and covered with dirt.

"What about the dogs?"

"Coyotes and buzzards will take care of them," Ben replied, turning toward the truck and opening the door.

With a shrug I secured my Remington in the window rack and hopped up into the cab. As I turned and drove back toward the road I looked into my rearview mirror. The eastern sky was a cool gray, and the stars were fading from view. Only charred remains occupied the space where the little house and stable had been. The old truck and tractor, both bullet riddled, would likely sit abandoned for years to come, and we would tell no one about the shallow graves or the men who had died so bravely. I suddenly felt overwhelmed by all the death I had seen and the killing I had done. A few days ago I thought I might live forever, and today I wondered how many minutes I had left. So fragile, so valuable, is this strange and sensational experience we call life.

Lost in our own ponderings we rode along in silence until we had returned to the highway.

"Seems strange to think of that little Comanche attack as a blessing." Ben broke the silence first, though he didn't look at me.

"A fuckin' blessing? I don't see it as any blessing. We nearly died, and those two men, Nara and Isatai, were having a pretty peaceful night until we showed up."

"Yes, it is an unfortunate thing for them, but death comes to us all, and they died good deaths. Besides, I don't think our showing up had anything to do with it, although I must admit it does seem oddly coincidental. It is likely Jacob would have had them killed for his own reasons, but if he knows we were there he'll know why, and he'll know we're coming. We can only hope he stays put long enough for us to reach him.

"But what I'm saying is that Isatai refused to help us initially. When Jacob came by here on his way south, seeking a place to raise warriors, Isatai had afforded him this information. In exchange Isatai expressed his wish to be reborn after his impending death despite the fact he no longer seeks revenge. Jacob refused him. Still Isatai was reluctant to help us because he held out hope that Jacob would change his mind. At the time I kept thinking to myself that he doesn't know Jacob. But now… Well I guess he knows Jacob the same way I know Jacob."

"You'd think he'd want to keep a few friends."

"No need for friends when your heart is filled with hatred and your soul obsessed with vengeance. It is a tortured and lonely existence fueled only by the hunger to kill. Let's hope we can end his tortured reign and his insatiable desire to kill."

"This place, Canyon del Rescate, I don't think I've ever heard of it." I had been going over locations in my head since Isatai had mentioned the location, and nothing had jumped out at me.

"Hmm. What about Casa Amarillo?"

"Now *that* I know something about. I went up there with my dad when I was just a kid. Matter of fact, I think I remember hunting around there."

"After what we saw tonight I'm guessing they're striking in far more places than we are aware. First they struck south of where you live and now this far north. My guess is that maybe Broken Spoke is the center of their wheel. You did say most of the people there are descendents of the original settlers."

"Yeah."

"This is far larger than just you, my friend. We best get them before they get what they're after. This is a big kill for Jacob, and I fear there are many lives at stake."

The gray light of dawn gave way to first light as the sun crept into the sky. Silence prevailed as the miles passed beneath us, and with the full light of morning we arrived at a desolate pit near Canyon Del Rescate.

🎇 **11** 🎇

Someone's been here recently; look at the fresh tracks." Ben observed.

I strained for a moment to decipher fresh marks in a roadway ahead of me as I nodded to Ben. Without another word we traveled for nearly a mile between short rows of brown-leaf Chinquapin oaks while my truck caressed the outer edges of cotton plants on either side of the narrow trace. In the distance yellow colored bluffs gleamed in the sunlight.

"If I remember correctly there's a huge pit further up this road. I was just a kid when we hunted here, but I remember the trees and it seems right to me."

Slowing my truck to cross yet another cattle guard, I spotted the filtered butt of a recently finished cigarette.

"You see that butt?" I asked.

"No. Where?"

I slowed as Ben leaped from the vehicle and followed my directions to the remnant.

"Jacob's brand." He snorted and dropped the butt back to the ground. "Let's go," Ben said as he returned to the truck and then quickly dialed his phone. "O'Reilly. Ben. We think we've located their base of operations. I'll text you the coordinates. Yeah, that's right. You're already heading for Broken Spoke? Okay, we'll wait for your arrival." Ben pulled the phone from his ear and returned it to the clip on his belt. "How much farther do you think?"

"I don't know for sure. I guess it's probably another quarter to a half mile, maybe."

"Let's park the truck and go in on foot from here."

"Should I pull it off the road?" I asked, referring to the vehicle.

"No. They have vehicles, and if they're in here I don't want them escaping."

Leaping from the vehicle I snatched the Remington off the rack again. Following Ben's lead I filled my other hand with my revolver. Weapons at the ready we walked along the dirt road toward the pit. We hadn't gotten far when a very faint rhythmic beating of drums and the high-pitched wailing of chants rose up to us. A spark of recognition showed in Ben's eyes, and he dropped into a crouch.

"They're here!" he hissed.

"What do we do?"

Again Ben punched a number into his phone, his demeanor focused, almost as though he were a cat approaching prey. "O'Reilly, we've definitely located them." Ben listened quietly while a barely detectable look of disgust betrayed itself in his features. "What are we supposed to do? You said you were en route when we talked earlier. How can you be that far away?"

Again he paused and listened. "We may not have time to wait for you and the task force. Mrs. Drake's life is in danger. They may already know we're here, and we may not have another chance to apprehend them if we don't act immediately." Ben scowled deeply shaking his head as he heard something he didn't like. "Fine, we'll wait, but you get here as quickly as you can, and tell that sheriff to have his men come in on foot, no sirens. And, O'Reilly... Tell them to be quick about it." Ben hung up. "Stupid bastard," he hissed.

"What now?" I asked.

"We need to see what it is we're up against. So let's move off to the right there and get into the cover of the cotton plants. We're going to have to wait until we have some backup. O'Reilly is at least an hour away, but he said he'll call the county and have the sheriff dispatch some of the local deputies. They should be here ahead of him."

With that, the two of us knelt and worked our way into the limited cover. Crawling on our stomachs, we slithered up to the edge of the pit. Looking down, I was amazed by what I saw. Seven men were dancing and chanting loudly forming a circle around a small altar where smoke rose from smoldering grasses. Each man wore an elegant, if not eerie, shirt. Decorated with a variety of quills, beads, blood and feathers, the long shirts covered them to mid thigh. Forming a larger circle around the center dancers a ring of another dozen warriors, some of them naked, others in various forms of modern dress, mimicked the same steps. I quickly identified Mohawk as one of the outer dancers. Then I noticed Scar Lip also in the circle. Two men sat beating a large drum sounding the same, rhythmic melody matched perfectly by the shuffling steps of the dance troupe.

Off to one side were two small tepees, aged and worn, and two older model pickup trucks. One pickup was a 1958 Chevrolet and the other a 1963 Ford. I scanned the area in an attempt to locate my mother. When I spotted her I boiled with fury. I was relieved to see her alive, but her condition was dreadful. She was sitting on the ground about ten yards from the lodges. Most of her clothing had been torn from her body, and she sat cowering in a fetal position with her arms around her knees and her face resting on her arms. One of her naked ankles was tethered to a stake in the ground. She lifted her head on occasion and looked about with wild, fearful eyes. The knifing pain in my heart caused a tear in my eye when I noticed that some of her hair was missing on the right side of her bloody head. The cuts and abrasions on her face, shoulders, arms, and legs caused my skin to crawl. One breast was completely visible while the other was covered by what remained of her shirt. Her loins were completely bare. I had never seen my mother nude and felt ashamed for her.

"Stinking bastards," I growled, twisting in a grip of anger and hatred as I fully realized the suffering she had endured at the hands of her ruthless captors. "We've got to get my mother! They are going to fuckin' die for whatever they've done to her."

"We'll get her, Brady. We will," Ben hissed, with urgency as he tried control my anger. "But they're all armed, and if they even think we're here they might just kill her. You've got to realize that no one wants them dead more than I do."

We lay silent for no less than ten minutes when one of the demons took the liberty to exit the circle. Grabbing a firebrand out of a smoldering cook fire, he skipped across the barren ground and jabbed the flaming poker into mother. She writhed at the end of the tether, wailing and struggling to move away from her abuser.

"Fucker!" I snarled and nearly leaped from the ground. Ben's hand pressed hard into my shoulders as the cackling bastard stalked off raising his hands to the sky and howling as though he had committed some brave act. I shrugged away from Ben's repressive hold as my mother's wailing sobs rose up out of the canyon.

"Brady…"

"I'm not going to lay here and watch them torture my mother."

"Neither am I."

"But you fuckin' are!"

"If anyone goes near her again you have my permission to shoot the bastard. Otherwise, we wait and go in just as soon as the deputies get here."

"They better get here quick."

"Listen to me. If we don't get Jacob then we can't kill them all. We'll need to take as many of the inner circle alive as we can. Jacob is the tallest man there in the center. So, whatever else happens, we either kill all *but* Jacob, or we need to capture one of the others there in the center wearing the shirts. If he escapes we need to capture as many as possible because Jacob Dark Moon isn't likely to go too far if we have some of his inner circle in captivity. The longer we can keep him nearby, the better chance we'll have to finally get the bastard. You got that, Brady?"

I glowered at him furiously and couldn't bring myself to agree.

"I'd like an opportunity to see if I can get confessions from them for some unsolved murders in the Dakotas. I also want to make sure Jacob hasn't taught others how to effectively perform the Ghost Dance. There are seven in that inner circle, which means they've taught at least one other person since my time with them. Used to be that only Jacob knew the secret as to how it works. Unfortunately, I won't know for sure until I have a chance to talk with some of them. So capturing some of that inner circle is very important. You with me on this, Brady?"

"Yeah, I reckon," I muttered spitting into the dust, "But if any of those fuckers touch my mother again I ain't going to care who I kill."

As I lay there watching my mother writhing in pain my anger festered, and I lost all sense of my surroundings. I became consumed with the desire to rush into the encampment and kill every last one of the Dancers and their spawn. And, although Ben's barely audible curse registered, it was the wail of a distant siren that shook me from my daydreams of murder. The increasing pitch told me that several vehicles were approaching. In another moment the tone reached the Dancers, and the circle broke immediately.

"Damn it! I said to have them come in quietly," Ben spat. "Get back to the truck, we've got to move. We're going to have to rush them. I'll kill as many of the warriors from the outer circle as possible; you focus on securing your mother."

Not really listening to anything Ben said other than that we were going to kill the sons of bitches I got onto one knee and aimed at the bastard who had burned my mother. I pulled the trigger and watched with great satisfaction as the bullet entered the demon's skull, and he fell dead to the ground where he had danced.

The echo of my rifle and the death of the warrior caused a barrage of gunfire to erupt from the pit below. Ben and I ducked instinctively as the air around us came alive with a hailstorm of bullets. Both of us broke into a dead run, stumbling on the uneven shrub-strewn ground, until we reached the truck and leaped into the cab. Shifting into gear, I stomped down on the accelerator, and the truck lurched forward kicking up dust from the hard dry earth. As we descended into the bowels of the impression, Ben pulled himself out through the open window and sat on the door frame. Men raced about the encampment grabbing up the altar, tossing gear into the trucks, and pulling down the lodges. Reaching for the weapons holstered beneath his armpits Ben grabbed his guns and unleashed a barrage of hot lead. His first volley dropped several Comanche warriors as they made attempts to reach my mother. Bearing down on her I pulled alongside and leaped from the vehicle. Having reloaded Ben continued firing relentlessly at the oncoming killers. Bullets whined all about me as I raced toward

Momma. I guess she was in a deep state of shock, because she didn't react to the chaos at all.

As I reloaded my Colt one warrior leapt toward me with a war club raised above his head. As the club descended towards my head I twisted away and, in one motion, slapped shut the fully loaded cylinder, aimed, and fired. The bullet got him between his large, black eyes just as the ball of the club glanced off the side of my skull. The impact staggered me, and I fell to the ground. Despite the blood running down the side of my face I felt little more than dazed from the blow. I suspect the adrenaline pumping through me shielded me from the pain. Struggling to my feet I glanced at Ben and caught his eyes getting a nod of response from the man. Holstering the pistol I turned to my mother.

I reached for her ankle as I fumbled my knife out of my back pocket. Slicing through the rawhide tether I scooped my mother into my arms and dashed back to the cab of the truck before stuffing her inside and leaping in.

I slapped the truck into gear as Ben slid into the cab. He had a fresh wound visible in his arm and a bloody crease alongside his head above the left ear. It seemed to me that the empty magazines hit the floor of the cab about the same time Ben slammed fresh ones into his pistols.

In that same instant bullets punched out the remains of my rear window, the passenger side mirror exploded, and holes appeared in the roof of the truck. We all hunched lower as the shower of hot lead raked the vehicle. Cutting the wheel hard left I stomped on the accelerator. Bearing down on the central mass of warriors and dancers I pointed the truck in the direction of the narrow roadway leading up and out of the pit.

Ben turned to look out the back window as glass and windshield exploded all around him, he bellowed. "Jacob!"

Ben fired with both weapons at once and bullets rained down on the men of the inner circle as they descended on my truck. The bullets from Ben's twin Glocks beat most of them back but didn't seem to puncture the shirts. It was almost like they were some sort of armor. During a pause Ben dropped back into his seat once again to reload.

Sensing something more was about to happen, I looked past Momma and directly at Swift. In a moment of surreal slow motion one of the shirted warriors landed on the side of the speeding vehicle.

Leaning into the cab he loosed a piercing war cry that echoed with the resonance of a thousand warriors. Fear and a sense of impending death rippled through me as the scream reverberated to the core of my soul. The chill running up my spine nearly paralyzed me, and for just a moment I let off the accelerator.

Dropping one of his weapons into his lap Ben wrestled with the man who managed to wrap the fingers of his right hand around Ben's throat. The powerful hand closed quickly constricting with such force I figured he would crush Ben's windpipe outright. Ben shook, struggling with his free hand to pry the fingers from his neck, while slipping his remaining hand up under the warrior's chin.

"Happy hunting, Bobby Red Crow," Ben rasped before pulling the trigger.

The roar of the gun was followed by a splatter of blood and brains on the roof of the cab, the wailing screams of my mother, and the immediate disappearance of Bobby Red Crow from the passenger window of my truck.

"One Dancer down, six to go." Ben gasped for breath and rubbed his bruised throat. In that same moment I know he realized, as I did, that the forces here were overwhelming, and we wouldn't survive if we stayed here in the pit. Ben hunkered down in the seat as he gesticulated towards the track we'd driven down to get here. "Go, Brady, go! Get up top!"

Catching a glimpse in the passenger side mirror of Bobby Red Crow's corpse bouncing on the hard dirt I bent low and focused again on my driving. Momma continued screaming, her body shaking and tears rolling down her face.

Suddenly a solid strike landed in my left ear. In the side mirror I saw the body of a devil-eyed Comanche perched in the bed of my truck. Ben, already aware of two more who had managed to leap into the vehicle, turned his weapon on them and emptied his magazine. A heartbeat later three bullet-riddled bodies toppled backwards out of the truck. With my ears ringing in tune with the throbbing of my skull I prayed like hell that we'd make it up the ramp.

Just as I topped the rise I veered to the right barely missing a head-on collision with an oncoming deputy sheriff's vehicle. Despite my best efforts my truck sideswiped the oncoming cruiser, and my truck fishtailed for a moment before I regained control. The collision caused the other vehicle to miss the roadway down into the pit and instead sent the cruiser careening over the edge of the fifteen-foot cliff.

I had no time to see the vehicle crash, but I heard it just as a second police car slammed into the rear quarter of my recovering truck. The impact of the cruiser righted my vehicle, sending us barreling straight down the dirt road.

"They need help," I gasped, applying the brakes and clutching the wheel with shaking fingers.

"Don't stop! Go! Go! Go, Brady!" Ben hollered. "We're outgunned, and I'm hurting bad."

Shrugging off the thought of assisting the officers I sped up and was shocked to feel the vehicle lurch forward. I glanced into the rearview mirror only to see the large front grill of a 1958 Chevrolet pickup truck as it slammed into the rear end of my truck. The three of us hunkered down as yet more bullets pounded the rear of the cab. For fear of exposure I could barely see over the dash from my current position.

Ramming me again, the men in the pickup truck howled and shrieked as one of them leaned from the passenger side window and fired a double-barreled shotgun loaded with slugs. Both rounds rocketed through the cab and struck what remained of the windshield sending a shower of glass across the hood. My mother's wailing intensified as she attempted to crawl down onto the floor.

"Sons of bitches," I yelped as I looked into the side mirror to see the Dancers and their offspring hard on my ass. I spotted a second truck, the other one from down in the pit, loaded haphazardly with the two lodges and personal gear. Both sped along single file right behind me.

"Whatever you do don't stop and don't go off the road. When you hit that pavement ahead, you head west until we meet up with the local cops, or O'Reilly and the other agents, or all of them."

"Okay, Ben, whatever you say," I hollered over the popping of gunfire and the endless screeching of my mother. "It's okay, Momma! You're going to be okay."

The truck behind us slammed my bumper a couple more times before we hit the main road. As I slowed down to turn onto the paved road Ben turned toward the rear of the truck. Extending both Glock-filled hands out through the glassless window he fired several shots into the windshield of the truck directly behind us. The vehicle veered into the cotton field, bounced around a bit, and was nearly mired in the vegetation and soil. The Ford pulled ahead while the Chevy struggled to get back onto the pavement.

"That ought to give them pause before they to ram us again," Ben said as he sat back down.

Driving as fast as I could with the windshield gone and veering back and forth to deny the assailants any opportunity to pull up alongside we made our way west.

"Damn it, I'm getting real low on gas," I shouted as a new level of panic wrenched on my guts. My mother's wailing had lowered to a subtle form of continuous sobbing as we raced along the highway. The trucks with the warriors in them were still behind us, but they were far enough back that they couldn't get off any damaging shots. Despite that they still intermittently sent rounds our way as if trying to remind us that they were still pissed as hell.

Suddenly the flashing lights of a half-dozen Texas Highway Patrol and County Sheriff cars appeared on the distant horizon. The two trucks following us slowed immediately and changed direction, and in a matter of seconds they were headed east at top speed.

"Turn around, Brady!" Swift barked.

"What for? Shit. Now?"

"Yes, now. You want to wait to deal with them on their terms or get it over with today? Let's catch them while we've got reinforcements!"

"Shit," I exclaimed again slowing the truck and cutting the wheel.

Skidding sideways before dipping into a crop field I pulled back onto the highway and gave chase. The faster, more agile police sedans closed quickly on us, and the voice of Sergeant Dickens barked orders to pull over his loudspeaker.

"Forget him, Brady. We've got criminals to catch," Ben snarled.

Pushing the truck for all it was worth I realized the Dancers and their pets were getting away, and the police were gathering around us working their cars in an attempt to encircle the truck and slow me down. Despite my best effort to outrun them, cruisers managed to surround me and I was forced to slow as their vehicles penned me in. Within moments four of the police cars and my truck came to a dead stop while two others continued in pursuit of the Dancer's vehicles.

"Damn fools," Ben hissed.

"Get out of the vehicle with your hands up," Patrolman Dickens's voice demanded over the speaker mounted in his grill.

Eyeing the half-dozen officers with their guns drawn and aimed at us I slowly got out of the vehicle with my hands in the air. My mother whimpered and sobbed. Unwilling, or maybe unable, to get out of the vehicle she simply attempted to cover her nearly naked body with the few strands of clothing left to her and fell over into a fetal position on the seat. Detective Ben Swift dropped the pistols on the floor of the truck, rolled out of the passenger side, and walked toward the rear of the vehicle with his fingers interlaced behind his head.

"Get down on the ground, now!" barked Officer Dickens.

Both Ben and I complied as several officers lunged forward. Racing up to us the officers fell on us. Cuffing our hands behind our backs the policemen yanked us to our feet.

"Got a naked woman in here!" shouted yet another officer as he stood with his weapon pointed into my truck, "No telling what these two must have done to her."

"That's my mother, you sick fuck," I bellowed, "and we just rescued her from the jackasses *you* let slip away. She needs medical attention. Now!"

The red, angry face of patrolmen Dickens appeared just inches from mine, his spittle lathering my face as he hissed, "You mind your manners when you speak to my officers, Mr. Drake. You're in enough trouble without adding resisting arrest and disrespecting a police officer to the charges."

"Fuck you, Dickens," I barked, adrenaline still rushing through my veins.

His nightstick cleared the holster and struck me up under my jaw just as I noticed the two black Chevy Suburbans pulling up behind the cruisers. Staggering backwards, my head pounding like a jackhammer, I slammed into the side of my truck and slid down into a seated position on the pavement.

"That's about enough of that, Sergeant, or you'll find yourself up on some charges of your own," Swift snarled as he eyed the man with undisguised loathing.

"You mind your own business, injun." Dickens turned and pointed his night stick in Ben's direction.

"Sad to see bigotry is still alive and perpetrated by some people. Why don't you pull your narrow mind out of your fat ass, Dickens?"

Patrolmen Dickens spun his nightstick and stepped toward Ben with sheer malice in his eyes. He lifted his hand and was about to give Ben some of the same treatment he'd just given me when men in suits poured from the Suburbans.

"Patrolmen, you back away from those men!" Federal O'Reilly shouted as he and several agents walked on the scene. The FBI agents stepped around the police officers effectively shielding us from any more abuse.

"Agent Winters, there's a woman in here. Grab a blanket, will you?" one of the men shouted. As another man helped me to my feet, a woman that I assumed to be Agent Winters went to the aid of my mother and guided her back to one of their vehicles.

After a heated discussion between O'Reilly and Patrolmen Dickens about jurisdiction and interference in a federal investigation the Highway Patrol stepped aside and left us in the custody of the federal agents. Several ambulances arrived, and two of them, accompanied by tow trucks, went on toward Canyon del Rescate to meet up with deputy sheriffs to recover the wounded officers there. Two others stopped behind the FBI vehicles. Swift and I were led toward them while one of the paramedics jogged to the Suburban where my mother rocked back and forth in the back seat. Paramedics worked quickly over Ben and me to dress our wounds and set up IVs. As I lay on the gurney, eyes closed and disconnecting myself from the stress of the past dozen hours, my head began to ache, and my injuries burned. They had barely settled us into our respective ambulances when both Ben and I began simultaneously protesting being taken to the hospital in Lubbock.

"It's for your own good," O'Reilly argued with Ben.

"We're fine," I yelled from my secluded perch inside the ambulance.

"We've got to get Jacob and the others *now*," Ben growled as he began tearing at the dressing and catheter in his arm.

"Sir, you are in no condition to—" protested one of the paramedics.

"I've been through worse."

"Well you're going to injure yourself a whole lot more if you rip that catheter out."

"Let them go." O'Reilly ordered from where he stood giving instructions to his field agents. He sounded resigned more than anything and a frustrated sigh accompanied his words.

"What?" The paramedic stared at O'Reilly incredulously, his hands still resting on Ben's shoulders.

"Let them go. It's their funeral. I have murderers to catch and potentially dozens of lives to save. If these two want to give theirs up to save others that's fine with me."

"But—" began Ben's attendant.

"If you don't want to be arrested for interfering with an FBI investigation let them go!" The frustration in O'Reilly's voice bubbled over, and he stared daggers at the man that was arguing.

Reluctantly, the paramedics disconnected us from their monitors and tubes. Within minutes we were both heading for my truck. We were about halfway there when O'Reilly intercepted us.

"You need to tone it down a bit, Swift. You put the lives of Brady and his mother in jeopardy with your reckless actions. Let me remind you that this is a Federal case, and you are here as a liaison with Pine

Ridge law enforcement and the Bureau of Indian Affairs. You are not the lead on this investigation!"

"I am the only one qualified to deal with this investigation. The FBI inserted itself into this mess after I'd been following it for weeks. You remember that!"

"Now you listen here, Detective—" O'Reilly began.

I didn't hear anything after that. Ben grabbed me by the arm and we stalked away from O'Reilly, and his message became lost in the din of engines and sirens as agents and police began leaving the scene.

As soon as we were seated in my truck with Ben behind the wheel I turned to him. "Ben, I know we need to catch Dark Moon, but I'd like to go to Levelland and see my mother. Besides, I feel like hell, and I don't think a little medical attention would hurt either of us."

Ben stared at me, portraying an intense darkness for a moment, but did not respond.

"I mean, well, I reckon we can head east if you want," I stuttered. The gaze unnerved me and reminded me too much of the Dancers for me to hold it, so I looked away.

Ben started the truck and we headed west. We had barely gone a mile when two Highway Patrol cruisers, the ones that had passed us in pursuit of the Dancers, passed us because, we would later learn, they had lost track of the trucks containing our suspects.

With a retinue of government servants traveling behind us, my head throbbing with pain, and Swift seated behind the wheel of my truck, we headed for Levelland. Not a word passed between us during our return trip to the hospital. After arriving, suffering through a few tests and getting patched up, I found Ben and we grabbed a quick bite to eat in the cafeteria. I needed that food more than anything else, I think, because microwave lasagna had never tasted so good. Ben and I passed by the reception desk and found the room where my mother was being treated. The attending nurse told me that she was to remain there for observation, given her ordeal and unstable condition. Standing in the hallway outside her room, I discussed her prognosis with Dr. Watson.

"So you think she'll be alright?"

"Physically, I suspect she'll make a full recovery. I've ordered a psych eval for her tomorrow. The trauma has taken its toll on her, and she may need some help recovering mentally."

Together we watched her through the glass partition as she rocked on her bed and mumbled to herself. Twice she yanked her own hair and cried out as though reliving moments of her tortuous captivity. At that moment I had to agree with her doctor; she needed to be evaluated and maybe see a shrink.

Momma burst into tears when I entered her room. Clutching me as though I were her life preserver in a sea of uncertainty she sobbed and shrieked while the torments of her recent past whirled in her mind's eye. I consoled her as best I could with reassuring words and, with doubt welling up in my heart, promised to keep her safe. As I held her I told her about how things would get better now that the Feds were involved and how we'd fix up the house all new like. Finally she stopped trembling and seemed to get herself together, but when I attempted to leave she began to wail and tear at the IVs.

Nurses rushed into the room, one bearing a sedative, but as they tried to administer it my mother attacked them viciously. After a few minutes of enduring the onslaught they called for help, and two male orderlies worked to restrain her. I couldn't stand to watch any longer.

"She wants to go home, Doc. Let me take her home," I bellowed over the sound of my mother's cries and the beeping of disconnected machines.

"She needs medical attention and a psych evaluation, Mr. Drake. I can't just let her go. She could do herself more damage."

Ben stepped into the doorframe, blocking the entrance of two security guards. His stern demeanor and beleaguered appearance had a profound effect on their desire to get involved.

"You have no right to keep her. She has the right to leave unless this hospital imprisons people against their will."

"Brady, I…"

"Doc, she's going with me. Now. I'll try to get her in tomorrow for a follow-up, but she's going home with me."

"Fine. You take her, but I will not sign off on her release. Let the record show that I protested this action, and that I strongly urge you to reconsider."

"There's nothing to reconsider. She'll get the care she needs, but I'm taking her home."

The doctor nodded his head to the nurses eyeing us. With his reluctant approval they began to prepare her for discharge.

Ben and I waited quietly in the hallway while the nurses dressed her in the clothes I purchased at the gift shop. Following the nurse who wheeled my mother outdoors to the parking lot we helped Momma up into the truck. Not a word was spoken amongst us as we drove out of Levelland and headed for home. The sun shone brightly and the air was warm, but within each of us were the dark clouds of foreboding and the bone chilling cold of our recent memories. Upon reaching Broken Spoke the two of us assisted Momma into the house. Ben went immediately to the back yard, and I stayed with Momma until she rested comfortably in her bedroom.

Now, as I sit completing this entry, it seems we'll have to find the Dancers and their warring horde all over again, or more than likely they'll find us when we least expect it.

Journal entry: September 04, 10:57 p.m. Today the circus came to town.

⁂ **12** ⁂

O'Reilly showed up late in the afternoon and posted two of his agents outside our house. I slept soundly feeling vaguely more secure, until early this morning.

When I woke in the predawn hours a light rain fell outside my window. Getting to my feet, I shuffled to the bathroom and slipped into the shower. I stood beneath the steaming spray, washed my wounded and aching body, and for a few moments felt removed from the world around me. But my thoughts soon returned to the mess that awaited me just beyond the thin shower curtain and the violence and pain that had entered my life and Momma's.

Overcome with a mixture of grief, fear, and regret, I sobbed quietly. Tears fell from my eyes and melded with the stream of water running over my face to run undetected into the drain below while subtle tremors wracked my body. I don't know how long I stood there, but when the water began to run cold I shut it off and stepped back into the world where my unforeseeable fate awaited me.

The rain ended just after dawn, and by midmorning the clouds had passed leaving the plains of northern Texas basked in the brilliance of the sun. The air warmed quickly, and the water that had fallen evaporated. While Momma slept I occupied myself with cleaning and making minor repairs to the house, and Ben mumbled something about going for a walk and stepped out the backdoor of the house.

The sudden shrill of Momma screaming shot a chill up my spine and my hand strayed to the .45 on my hip. I ran for her bedroom to find her thrashing about in her bed.

"Momma! Momma, calm down." I worked feverously to restrain her. "Momma, you're going to hurt yourself."

She continued to spasm in a fit of rage and fear as I dialed the phone.

"Doc? Yeah, Brady. Thank God you're home. Momma is in a bad way and I'm afraid she's fix'in to hurt herself."

"I'll be right there."

"Thanks, Doc."

I continued to try and calm her as the minutes ticked by. Being a neighbor and living just two streets west of ours Doctor Watson arrived at the house a few minutes later. As I held her down the doc gave Momma a sedative.

"She is going to need some professional counseling," he told me, "and possibly spend some time in Lubbock for observation."

"Yeah, I can see that."

"Brady," he said with a stern look, "you be sure to keep that appointment I gave you for the psych eval."

"I will, Doc, I will."

The two of us stood over her until the sedative had done its work, and Momma lay quietly propped up on her pillows.

"I'm headed to Levelland to make my rounds. Give her one of these every four hours to keep her calm. I'll check back with you later."

I took the small plastic bottle of pills from the doctor. "Thanks, Doc. Sorry to pull you away from your duties."

"No problem, Brady. Just take care of your mother. I'll talk with you later."

I showed the doctor out and went back to the chores at hand. I cut a piece of plywood and fashioned a door for the bathroom, cleaned up Rufus' body and the blood associated with it, and cleared away the debris caused by bullets passing through the walls of the house during the gun battle. I found a partial bucket of drywall mud in the shed and filled all the holes I could find.

Taking a look around I felt satisfied that the house was now returned to a state of near normal. I took a quick look at Momma, who slept soundly beneath the quilt wrapped around her body, and stepped outdoors.

"You guys need anything?" I asked the agents seated in the front seat of their sedan.

"No thanks, we're all set," one replied.

"I'm fix'in to run a small errand, do you mind keepin' an eye on my mom?"

"No problem."

"Great, thanks. I won't be long."

Stepping around the corner and crossing the backyard I squatted down and scooped up the blanket holding Rufus' remains. Clutching a shovel in my right hand I stepped into the alley and made my way to Main Street. Walking two blocks I reached the edge of town and stopped just outside the graveyard next to the railroad tracks. I lay Rufus on the ground, dug a hole four feet deep, and then laid his body to rest.

"Dear God, or anyone listening, please bless this poor critter. He was a short-lived friend who gave his life trying to protect my Momma. Amen"

I filled the hole and marked it with a few dry, reddish-violet blossoms from a nearby autumn sage bush. With the shovel slung across my shoulders I headed toward home. As I walked past Benny's I decided some beer wouldn't be a bad thing right now. I stepped around back and rapped on the door.

"*Quien es*?" sounded Benny's familiar greeting.

"Brady."

The door opened and I stepped inside. Pulling some cash from my pocket I bought a case of Lone Star beer and returned to the house. After checking on Momma I slid three six-packs into the fridge and tossed the other into a small cooler and filled it with ice.

By the time the rest of the Feds arrived I had planted my ass on the front porch of our house. Seated just six inches from my mother's partially open bedroom window with my back against the wall I was seeking solace in the cold Lone Star pouring down my throat.

It was well past midday when the motor home pulled into my yard and parked in the shadows cast by the trees along the southern edge of the driveway. Adorned with government plates and a series of dishes and antennas it was obvious to me that the Federal Bureau of Investigation had officially arrived in Broken Spoke. That fact began to draw the attention of my neighbors as they set up their little circus in my front yard. Drinking my beer, and drowning out the demons in my mind, I was happy for the distraction. And maybe it was the beer, along with the fact that I hadn't eaten, but I found myself entertained watching nearly a dozen federal agents set up their mobile headquarters.

As the crew rushed about plugging things in, setting up satellite dishes, monitoring equipment, and running tests I was grateful to be doing absolutely nothing. Each swig of beer tickled my senses as the alcohol flooded my bloodstream. I chuckled to myself as I came up with anecdotes like: *'They have a six-pack setup; I can drink a six-pack in the time it takes them to set up.'*

I first thought the government was going to station a small garrison of agents at our house, though I soon realized that most of the agents were here just to assist in the installation. As the waning shadows cast by the dying twilight were losing their grip on the north Texas plains the installation crew climbed into their black Chevy Suburbans and bid farewell to the other agents. Only two men and a woman remained at the house to work with Swift. O'Reilly stayed along with Agent Scott Nielsen and Agent Marlene Winters.

Fresh out of the academy, Agent Nielsen appeared to be a bit smug. Even more so than O'Reilly. His blond hair, blue eyes, and fit physique made him look like a college jock or a wayward surfer who had ventured inland from the beaches of California. My initial impression was that he'd lived a life of privilege and wasn't used to roughing it.

The third agent, Agent Winters, was anything but unpleasant to look at. Her dark eyes were piercing and seemed to take in everything, and her ebony skin warmed like polished mahogany in the orange light of the setting sun. She was definitely fit, her muscular physique evident through her business attire, and although very pleasant to talk to, I sensed an underlying intelligence beneath the rugged, street-wise demeanor.

As the light faded the three agents completed some finishing touches to their temporary home and office. O'Reilly walked over to the tree line and spoke briefly with Swift.

Ben had been unusually quiet all day. When he'd returned from his walk he borrowed my truck and was gone for a short while. When he got back he retreated to an old metal chair secluded in the shadows of the trees and had since sat there staring at the distant horizon and smoking cigarettes. He'd only briefly acknowledged the agents when they arrived and acknowledged me only when accepting the cold beer I had offered him.

When Agents O'Reilly and Nielsen disappeared into the large motor home Agent Winters wandered over to the edge of the porch. Shedding the blazer from her blouse-covered shoulders she sat down on the edge of the porch and laid it across her lap.

"Got any more of those, cowboy?" she cooed, indicating my beer.

"Yes, ma'am." Leaning over I reached down into the cooler next to the porch. I was prepared to sit right here until I was completely hammered. Retrieving a cold bottle from what remained of the ice I slid the lid back atop the cooler and sat upright. Quickly popping the top I leaned forward and offered the bottle to her.

"Thank you," she said in a southeastern twang.

"Where you from?" I asked.

"Georgia." She took a sip of the cold brew. "Just north of Atlanta."

"What d'ya think of Texas?"

"I like it," she said, swallowing more beer.

"Best damn place in the world."

"Is there a Texan who *doesn't* feel that way?" she asked, her flawless teeth shining through her full and smiling lips.

"No, probably not," I chuckled. "If there is they ain't a true Texan."

"And you? Are you a true Texan, Mister Drake?"

"Born and bred right here, ma'am. Truth is, except for crossing the border into New Mexico and a couple of jaunts into Oklahoma, I've never been anywhere but Texas. Can't imagine going anywhere else. But then, if you got the best, who needs the rest?"

She laughed along with me. It was a tender laugh, one that I sensed came easily to her.

"Seems this ordeal has rocked your little piece of heaven," she observed after a few moments.

Belching loudly after finishing my tenth beer and reaching for my eleventh I considered her observation for a moment before speaking. "Yes, ma'am, it sure has."

She said nothing. Although I didn't think on it at the time I suspect it was her way of fishing for details by giving me an opportunity to fill the silence and maybe offer something about the case the authorities didn't already know. Whatever her intentions I was just inebriated enough not to question her motives, and I felt a desire to talk.

"I guess the pain my Momma's been through is the hardest part of it. But I got to tell you I think I'm fixin' to go plumb *loco*. Despite the bad things I've seen I still can't shake the image of that first girl I saw. What happened to her haunts me something fierce. I mean *damn*. She was pretty and smiling, and if you could have *seen* that whirlwind wrap around her and heard those horrible noises before that heathen bastard stepped out of that thing you'd have about crapped your pants. I know I just about did. I mean I was so fuckin' scared, my nuts..." Feeling slightly embarrassed I shut my mouth and took a swig from my beer. "Sorry, ma'am, I didn't mean to say that."

"No apology necessary, Mr. Drake. I've got three brothers, all jocks, and there isn't much I haven't heard," she responded with a knowing grin. A slightly uncomfortable silence seemed to me to be her request for more information.

"Well, my Momma taught me better manners." I ignored my swelling emotions and returned to my unfinished story. "I just couldn't believe my eyes. And that damn devil! I call him Scar Lip because he's got a lip on his scar... Ah, shit," I said, laughing, "beer's talking. I meant to say he's got a *scar* on his *lip*."

Winters remained silent though she was grinning in response to my error, a real grin, nice, and pleasant like.

"Anyway, he just came after me. And he killed that old man behind the counter. Killed him like it was nothing. I know he would have killed me if I hadn't managed to escape. I hate that fuckin' Scar Lip. He tried to kill my mother, and he murdered poor Donny Jones. Then he showed up at the Morales place with Mohawk and Claw Fingers and another one… They killed those nice folks, too. What harm did those folks ever do anyone? None at all, that's what. They were just nice people, trying to live their own lives."

The smile faded from her lips as Agent Winters took a sip from her beer and considered my words. Her eyes focused on me with a benign intensity. "I didn't see any of this in the police reports, Mr. Drake. You told them you knew nothing about the incidents at Ten Mile Fork or at the Morales lease. Why would you do that? Why would you tell them you knew nothing if you have nothing to hide? And, based on your prior statements, why should I believe what you're saying now? You've got to admit this sudden confession is a bit suspect. After all, you've been drinking, and I have to say I've never heard a more sensational story. I think maybe the shock and the beer have tampered with your mind, Mr. Drake."

I stared at her for a moment not sure if she was calling me a liar or feeling sorry for me. I suspected it was both. I looked into her seductive eyes and decided it didn't matter either way. I sipped my beer and took some time to recollect myself before I replied.

"Yeah, your buddy in there, O'Reilly, don't believe a word he's been told about these dust devils either. But he will. I'm sure he will. And if I was you, Agent Winters, I'd be believing in what I tell you. It's probably the only chance you have of not ending up…"

I thought of the blond at Ten Mile fork and pictured the possibility of what might happen to Agent Winters. I downed the rest of my beer and just looked at the woman. I didn't want to think about it. Instead, I let my eyes wander down her body. Moments later, to my surprise, another emotion began to take over. I think she noticed the change in my demeanor and saw my eyes as they followed the contours of her female form. "Damn you look pretty, Agent Winters," I said, smiling and attempting to catch her eyes with mine.

"Me? Uh, Mr. Drake, I think that's your 'beer talking' again, and it's getting the better of you." Glancing at me briefly she stood and immediately walked in the direction of the trailer, leaving her partially empty bottle of Lone Star on the porch next to where she had been sitting. "We'll talk more tomorrow. We both need to turn in and get some sleep."

As she moved across the lawn my eyes focused on her fine ass and narrow waist. My fantasy was interrupted by the voice of reality. "He's right, Agent Winters. Your only chance of not ending up a victim is to begin this investigation with a belief in all of what he's told you." Swift's voice floated out from the shadows where he sat. "These stories are real, very real, and the specters have little on their minds but revenge. They are chosen for their ire, their restless need for vengeance. We must find the Ghost Dancers if we are to stop the process, but you might want to keep an eye out for whirlwinds of any size."

"Swift, I'm as open-minded as the next person," she answered, stopping midway between the porch and the motor home. Shifting her attention to the shadowed figure seated amongst the trees Agent Winters scowled. "But I'm for keeping things real, and I've never worked on any case that didn't end up proving to be just what it was. I am sure when we've caught these boys you call Ghost Dancers, or Shadow Dancers, or whatever you say they are, that there will be a very logical explanation.

"The Bureau utilizes proven scientific methods and solid physical evidence to solve its cases. And, truth be told, Detective, I've been involved in several cases where people claimed it was UFOs, or the Devil, or voices in their heads, that made them do terrible things. It always turns out that they were just sick, misguided fools making up stories to excuse themselves from what they've done. When this is all said and done a logical explanation will be provided, and you and Mr. Drake will feel a bit foolish. I'm surprised, you being an experienced lawman and all, that you would buy into this bunk."

Ben said nothing for a minute that seemed to stretch out into eternity. The sounds of the night filled the void. When no response came from the shadows Agent Winters turned and continued walking toward the trailer. She paused for a moment and reached for the door. The opening of the door cast light across the ground, and it was at that moment that Ben spoke again.

"Sleep well, Agent Winters. I've no doubt you'll have your proof, and I hope you get the opportunity to feel foolish."

Agent Winters hesitated for a second and shook her head before stepping inside. The door closed separating the agents from the rest of the world and likely from any chance of heeding Ben's warning.

❊ **13** ❊

The sound of loud voices brought me around the corner of the house. Recognizing the beginning of an argument I'd dropped my hammer and left my repair of the back door. Despite the early hour the sun was bright, and the air was already as hot as the tempers flaring in my front yard.

Sheriff Baker and Deputy Dawson were in a heated discussion with Eddie while the FBI agents simply looked on.

"Two more attacks," murmured Ben Swift rising from the ground where he had, once again, been inconspicuously seated in the shade of the trees. "One last night, and another this morning. Seems your wallet was found at one of them."

"What?" I said reaching for my back pocket only to discover my wallet wasn't there. Together we approached the group of lawmen.

"I don't give a damn what you say, Eddie. Every time one of these attacks occurs Brady Drake's either found in attendance, or there is evidence that he was," insisted Deputy Dawson.

"But ya'll have it wrong. He's been here since yesterday afternoon! I can vouch for that as can everyone else here. I've been helping him repair his back door since dawn," Eddie protested.

"Then how the hell do you reckon his wallet ended up over at the Cook residence? The entire family is missing, and the ranch house burned to the ground. His wallet was found right in the driveway next to the tire imprints from his truck. Those same tire tracks were found outside a phone booth in Morton where a young boy disappeared this morning. Now how do you explain *that*?"

"He never left the house," stated Swift.

"And why the hell should I buy what you're selling?" Sheriff Baker turned his gaze to the detective. "You were with him the day before yesterday when all that shit went down out there near Slaton. There are several deputies in the hospital thanks to you two. The perpetrators absconded, and all you've offered in this case is your bullshit stories about some damn dirt-devils."

"Dust devils," I corrected with a note of sarcasm in my voice. "A Dirt Devil is a damn vacuum cleaner."

"Don't start with me, Drake, you son-of-a-bitch," Sheriff Baker growled, taking two steps in my direction. "I think it's time you come on in with us. I've got a hankerin' to believe that if we take you out of circulation for a while this bullshit will stop."

Eddie stepped between the sheriff and me. Sheriff Baker glared at him momentarily but didn't continue his approach.

"Sheriff, Drake is instrumental in our efforts to catch these men," O'Reilly interjected. "I disagree with the way Swift and Mr. Drake have taken things on themselves, and I empathize with you in regards to the injuries sustained by your officers. However, I don't believe Mr. Drake is responsible for these crimes. Now, I agree that your evidence puts him awfully close to this recent series of events, but in spite of your circumstantial evidence I don't believe he's actually committing these crimes.

"Agents Nielsen, Winters, and I stayed up in shifts all night, and I can tell you that Mr. Drake did not leave the premises in any way that was apparent to us. His vehicle was here all night, and he's been here since his first cup of coffee at about 5:30 this morning. Since then he's been performing repairs to his house. And besides, from the looks of his truck, it isn't likely he'd get too far without a law enforcement officer pulling him over for questioning."

Everyone glanced at my windowless, bullet riddled pickup. Sheriff Baker simply shook his head in both disbelief and disgust.

"Now Sheriff, I don't buy their ghost story any more than you do. But I *do* believe we're chasing down some very bad men and that they are committing these crimes. I don't think Mr. Drake is a part of it, but he seems to have attracted their attention. Because of that we need him here on the ground where he'll attract the perpetrators to us. I don't know what it's all about, but they seem to want him awful bad."

"Well, O'Reilly," Sheriff Baker said with a hint of sarcasm, "I'll leave this young buck in your keep, but if he as much as farts in the wind ya'll better believe I'll be asking you what it smelled like."

With that, Sheriff Baker and Deputy Dawson returned to their cars and backed out of the yard leaving a cloud of dust. I turned about, shrugging and shaking my head in disbelief, and walked back around the end of the house to continue with my repairs. It seemed to me that the Dancers and their dauntless band of killers would stop at nothing to bring me down.

"I'm fixin' to pop over to my house and then run a few errands, Brady, but if you need anything you give me a jingle on my cell. I'll be back here at some point to check on you and your mom," Eddie said as he patted me on the shoulder and continued walking across my backyard toward the alley. His house was across the alley and one street over, clearly visible from my backyard.

"Do you think you can get my wallet back?" I called, taking a few steps after him and raising my voice.

"I suspect they'll want to keep it for evidence, but I'll ask."

"Thanks, Eddie. Thanks for standing up for me here this mornin' and for keeping an eye on things."

"No problem. As to the bullshit Baker is trying to stick you with all I can say is that damn Sheriff ain't stickin' you with a crime they can't solve just to try and close the books on it. Not on my watch," Eddie said sounding like an officer of the law for the first time since his appointment four years earlier. Crimes here in Broken Spoke were restricted to one or two domestic disputes per year, some traffic violations, and a few pranks by school kids during homecoming weekend. Ugly as it is, he was now involved in a real crime, and I think he kind of liked it.

I have to say that Eddie was a good egg and made a better lawman than most of the jerks serving in the Sheriff's department. He just never saw himself as being a patrolman or deputy sheriff, I guess.

But when the old constable retired and moved to San Antonio, Eddie volunteered for the job. And at this moment, I was damn glad he had.

With a wave and a nod we parted company, and I returned to repairing the damage done a few of days before. Hammering the outside molding back into place and reinstalling the screen door I completed the repair to my satisfaction. I returned the chop saw, my toolbox, and the electrical cord to the tool shed and locked it up tight before I headed inside to check on Momma.

Sitting quietly with her arms wrapped around her knees Momma looked like a small child in her long, white nightdress. Her hair hung loosely about her face, and she hummed softly as she rocked gently to and fro.

"How you doin', Momma?"

Her eyes remained fixed on the window, focused on the sun climbing in the distance, and she continued to hum as though I had said nothing. Unsure of her mental state, but glad to see her in a state of contentment, I turned to walk away. I hesitated when she answered without shifting her gaze. "I'm fine, Brady. I'm quite fine."

Her answer took me aback; it wasn't what I expected to hear. It wasn't her words but rather the tone of her voice along with an aura of serenity. I wondered if she was still sane or if the trauma of the recent events had stripped her mind from her.

"Are you sure, Momma? I mean you went through an awful lot the past couple of days."

"Yes, dear, I'm sure."

Although I felt that she wanted to tell me something an awkward silence settled between us. I stood there in her room, waiting, listening to the ticking of the alarm clock beside her bed, and when no words came I decided that maybe she wanted to be alone with her thoughts. I reckoned maybe she'd rather continue this conversation later so I turned once more to leave the room.

She cleared her throat and I stopped short. When I turned back our eyes met, and she looked at me in the way someone might look on a stranger. Her eyes softened, she became pale, and I felt her apprehension. She struggled for a moment before her lips quivered, and she spoke softly.

"He said you murdered his mother, Brady. He said you killed her right in front of him after you dragged her naked from her bed. He tore away my clothing and dragged me across the ground and beat me with a large stick. Then he took a knife to my scalp and started cutting. He pulled my hair out of my head when I resisted."

She trembled, and my heart went out to her, but she held up her hand when I took a step in her direction.

"He kneeled on my body and slapped me in the face. The whole time he glared into my eyes and screamed at me saying he was going to kill me right in front of you so that you'd know how it felt to see your mother murdered. He hurt me somethin' awful after that." She stared at me like she wanted an answer, but I was dumbfounded.

"Damn it, Brady, he raped me! And then they held me down while some of his men raped me!" Her voice strained with pain and anger while tears streamed down her face. "He just kept saying I deserved the same thing you and some others did to his mother. He hurt me because of what *you* did, Brady!"

"I didn't hurt anyone, Momma," I heard myself whine, almost by reflex, feeling very much like a child being accused of wrongdoing. My throat closed, and I couldn't force any more words out as my mind raced through all the discussions, all the things that had happened, and the dreams. I couldn't console Momma, but I couldn't walk away. So I stood frozen in her presence, while she reclaimed her composure.

"Were you there? Did you and your friends hurt his family, Brady? 'Cause he said you did terrible things, and his anger was real. It was damned convincing."

"What? Who said that?"

"Jacob, that Indian named Jacob."

"Jacob Dark Moon? The leader of those Dancers?"

"Yes, him. He said it, and he seemed awfully sure of it."

"Momma, you know me. I couldn't hurt anyone, and I certainly wouldn't have been near any killin'. Well, that is, until all this started. Goddamn it, what the hell is he talkin' about?"

"Maybe his mother was at that gas station down Ten Mile Fork way or something."

"Momma, I didn't kill the people at that gas station or anywhere else. Jacob Dark Moon's mother died over a hundred years ago shot to death by the U.S. Cavalry, and I…"

I became lost and confused in that moment, thinking again of my dream, remembering what Benjamin Swift said about past lives and spiritual memory. Maybe my ancestor, or a prior manifestation of myself, had been present at that raid where Jacob Dark Moon's mother was killed. I didn't know what to think. It was all too surreal and too strange for me to accept. In that moment I wanted only to forget and deny the possibilities presented.

"I… I didn't do it," I stammered, finally finding my voice, "and I don't care what he said. I can't believe you would take his word over mine. You must think very ill of me to even consider it."

But my brain churned slowly. I was caught between the dreams in my past and the memories of the immediate present. Despite my denial a shadow of doubt lingered in my soul stirring up memories and guilt for crimes committed. But it wasn't me. Not the me I know.

"I don't think ill of you, Brady. I'm just tellin' you what he said."

Stepping forward, I knelt beside her bed. "I'm sorry he hurt you. I am so sorry for not protecting you and for all the pain this has caused you. I hate myself for bringing this into your life. You didn't deserve any of this, and I just want things to be normal again."

She must have felt my sincerity and anguish, and she reached out and touched my face with her loving hand. "I'm okay, Brady. The day they took me, like every day since Roger died, I felt a bit lost. Now, don't get me wrong, I love you and look forward to you coming home every night and to fixing you coffee every morning, but I've felt lost for a long time. I've sat here wondering what my life is all about and wishing something would happen to make my days a little more meaningful.

"I guess the good Lord answered my prayers. It wasn't exactly what I had in mind, but he made me realize what a joy it is to sit here each day in the monotony of this town.

"After doing some thinking I realize we do what we have to do. I never would have suspected you would face death like that, to save me. You and the detective were very brave. I know now that we all have to be brave, and do the things we know need doing, regardless of our fears.

"I know I'm rambling, but I've a mind to move up to Oklahoma City with my brother. He's invited me to live with him and Ellen. So, I guess what I'm saying is it's time for me to do what I want to do. I've lived for you for a long time, and I could have died yesterday. And I ain't quite ready to die, Brady."

A single tear slipped down her face, and although her composure changed only slightly her aura of vulnerability caused me to lean toward her. I reached for her with a desire to comfort her. "Momma, I…"

She resisted my attempt to wrap my arms around her. For a moment I felt slighted, unaccustomed to any form of rejection by her. Until today I had never experienced it. Backing away from her I stood up.

"Now, Brady, ya'll be fine. You are a grown man, and you have your own life to live. I've got a life to live too. I've decided I'm going to Oklahoma."

In that moment I experienced a reversal of roles, and it felt as though I was the parent and she the child who was suddenly declaring her independence. As I stood looking down at her she appeared to me as though she were a young girl, both fearful and determined to push out into the world.

"Okay, Momma. I'm fine with that," I said softly.

It was then that she broke as she looked up at me with her body convulsing and tears streaming uncontrollably from her eyes. Feeling her need for closeness I sat down beside her and pulled her to me. She wrapped her arms around me and wept with her face pressed firmly against my shoulder. Sobbing, her body shook and the tension from the days before, from a lifetime of pain and silent anguish, released itself from her mind, body, and soul.

"It's okay, Momma. It's going to be okay," I repeated as we rocked for what seemed like an hour. I stroked her head and held her in my arms.

I think I changed inside, just a little, in that moment as her life came into focus for me. And the intimacy of that moment along with the fear of all that I had recently witnessed and didn't understand overtook me and slipped out of me in the form of tears. I guess I realized with some clarity that neither of us would be the same ever again.

When our emotions had exhausted themselves I leaned over and kissed her gently on the cheek, and she took my face in her hands.

"I love you, Brady," she whispered.

I stood, letting my hand fall from her shoulder. My desire to have a moment alone bubbled up from deep within my chest. I needed time to consider everything and to recover from the questions racing through my mind.

"I love you too, Momma. We'll get you moved up to Uncle John and Aunt Ellen's if that's what you want."

Turning, I walked across the room, and as I stepped through the door she said something very odd.

"I think I should have gone yesterday, Brady."

Turning back, struck by the oddness of her words and tone, I looked at her. For a moment, I was enraptured by the vision of her. Sitting there, she looked very much like the tiny child she once was with her bare feet tucked up under her legs. Bathed in the rays of sunshine streaming through the window an aura of gold and white light shrouded her entire being. Her face was cocked slightly to one side as though she was listening to sounds distant and difficult to hear, and she nodded in agreement to her own thoughts.

The beauty of an angel, I thought.

"What do you mean, Momma?"

She didn't respond right away, and I stepped through the open bedroom door and moved toward the kitchen, intent on getting a glass of water. She spoke in that moment. Stopping in mid-stride, I turned back to listen. "It's too late, my dear. It's too late for us all." Her voice was so soft and carried such finality with it that I couldn't make myself respond.

When she said nothing more I turned away and made my way to the kitchen. Her words sent a chill up my spine. Grabbing a glass from the cupboard I downed a glass of water and moved toward the door to the outside. I needed to take a walk to get away from everything.

Heading into the backyard I discovered the three agents from the FBI sitting around our picnic table discussing strategy. Between cell phone calls and punching up data on their notebook computers they sat plotting ways to draw the criminals out, referencing examples from crime solving textbooks, past experiences, expert theories, and criminal profile histories, all in hopes of conceiving a successful strategy for catching the Dancers. I just shook my head as I walked away. From what I heard of their chatter their rational strategies didn't seem to have any value in this surreal world.

Ignoring them I crossed the backyard, alley, and stepped out onto the street. As I walked across town my mind ran amuck with crazed thoughts of who I might have been or what I might have done. Without really thinking about it, I made my way toward the railroad tracks and sat on the wooden rail fence that surrounded the Broken Spoke Cemetery. Here, on the outskirts of town, amidst acres of tall grass, I had often found solace in the company of the dead.

Staring out across the prairie I wrestled with all that had happened. I pondered the plausibility of Ben's tale and of what I'd witnessed along with things I'd done. Despite my best efforts I couldn't make it fit with what I knew of the world before that run-in at Ten Mile Fork. I couldn't blame police for suspecting my involvement, and I couldn't blame the FBI agents for not believing the things Ben and I had told them.

One minute my mind was a blur of memories and dreams, and the next it was clear with the realization. People from all walks of life suffer from the residuals of atrocities, trespasses, indiscriminate acts of neglect, and selfishness that occurred generations ago. Across religious, ethnic, ideological, social, and gender lines people have been committing such acts against one another since human time began.

For the first time in my life I became aware that what I do each day can have lasting effects on those around me. Maybe not just in the short term but for generations to come. Suddenly I understood how important my individual life is in relation to the world at large and that if I want to change the world I must accept change within.

I know now that there are no ordinary people, no unimportant souls, and no individual persons on this planet on whom an act of cruelty or kindness is committed that does not affect human kind as a whole. Like a pebble in a pond we are all affected by the ripples it makes no matter where we are in the great body of this universe. We are one. And despite our beliefs or differences we are all reliant on one another in this quest, this experience, we call life. Your life, my life, is good or bad dependent upon how we treat ourselves and how we act toward and treat one another.

I felt a joy I have never known. It was as though for the first time I understood something about life that millions of people had never understood. In that moment I learned a primary lesson about life. Maybe this lesson is one we must suffer and learn to truly experience life. With tears running down my face I understood that my soul was immortal and that life truly has meaning. I wished I could share the joy I felt in those few moments, and maybe one day I can.

But as I sat there, staring out across the great land and sky of Texas, I knew that the moment could not last. Reluctantly I slid from atop the fence rail and turned toward home. With a wistful longing for my past I breathed in my hometown, and I reveled in its uniqueness and familiarity as I made my way along the main street looking at each vacant storefront and aged building. I reminisced about a time when businesses prospered here, and I was young.

I remembered when my daddy took me for my first real haircut in Buster's Barber Shop when I was four years old. Buster is now long dead, and the faded striped pole on the brick wall outside is all that remains of the barbershop. And over there, across the street, there used to be a little drive-in where you could get burgers, hot dogs, and ice cream. That place closed the same year I graduated from high school. These places are all shadows of the past much the same way these dust devils are, I guess.

Turning down East Street I passed J.J. Jackson's house and remembered our years of friendship. I wondered if his ancestors had anything in common with mine in regards to the Comanche and sincerely hoped that they didn't. I passed another half dozen houses before I stepped into my front yard and looked at our small home with great affection and appreciation.

At that moment I made a solemn oath to myself. I swore that when this is over I would strive to be a better person and treat all people with kindness and respect. I would assist them whenever I could and not hesitate to attempt to inspire others to be better in their acts toward one another. I believe that life on earth can be as idealistic as the concept of heaven if we all act as angels.

✳ 14 ✳

Your government tax dollars at work," Ben Swift quipped as I approached the agents seated at the back of the house. I'd given no thought to Ben's whereabouts but was immediately reminded of how he favored the lawn chair beneath the trees along the edge of the driveway. Had he not spoken it's likely I would've just grabbed my coffee cup and gone back inside. You know, as I'm writing, I think the coffee cup is still there.

"Hey, Ben," I said, pulling up short. "Do you reckon they're gonna catch'em before anything else happens?"

"I think they could if they had any idea what it is they're up against. I think we're still on our own. We're not only burdened with the task of catching the Dancers, but we're also the primary focus of their animosity at the moment. Killing Bobby Red Crow only served to rile them up. He was one of the original Dancers, and they're going to miss him terribly. He was probably the most resourceful person I ever knew. When the group wanted or needed something that little thief would not only locate it, but he'd be damn sure to bring it back."

"I can see where losing a guy like that might just piss them off."

"That and the fact that he's Jacob Dark Moon's brother."

"Jacob's brother?" My eyebrows lifted as I moved over, taking a seat in the chair next Ben. "Yeah, that probably would make him all the madder. My mother just talked about the bastard this afternoon."

"Jacob?"

"Yeah. She said that when he was beating her he told her he was going to kill her right in front of me, so as I'd know what it was like to see my mother killed. He told her I was the one who raped and killed his mother which is some crazy ass bullshit."

171

"Yeah, I remember that the top enlisted man that day was Sergeant Major Drake. Whether you believe it or not, you, or some part of you, must have been there that day. If Jacob says you were there then I would say you were there. It makes sense now. Damn, you're battling ghosts all up and down the plains, Brady Drake."

"Jacob Dark Moon saying it don't make it so," I growled. Despite my recent enlightenment I was still plagued by doubt swirling within me. No man changes in an instant, and deep down I was still angry that my life had been interrupted. For several minutes I was lost in thought struggling to come to terms with my return to this insane situation. I think I missed part of what Ben was saying because I abruptly realized that he was talking.

"Jacob Dark Moon is the most formidable man I've ever known; he can track a spirit better than a bloodhound can track a rabbit. He comes from a long line of Holy Men and is in tune with the spirit world. He uses it to fuel his hatred. It's his anger for what happened to his people, to our people, that keeps them all going.

"Some of the others have requested they use the dance to bring back some of the great leaders. When I was with the group we tried to persuade Jacob to bring back some of the wise and loving leaders of our tribe. We argued that they could help guide our people toward a better future and guide us in better use of this power. I told him our warriors failed then and will fail now. War is not the way. It is the best and brightest of our people who could navigate through the system and bring a better future to the People.

"Jacob fears bringing back leaders of any power because it might mean he has to relinquish some of his own. He fears they might seek to use the Ghost Dance to achieve what it was originally intended for or that he might be cast aside as more of our people return, and the peaceful and loving will of the People is considered in the use of the ghost shirts and the power of the dance."

"But what's the attraction to the constant killing? Doesn't he ever tire of it?"

Ben pulled a pack of smokes from his shirt pocket and tapped the open end lightly on the palm of his other hand. Several cigarettes slipped through the opening, and he raised the pack to his mouth and lodged one in his lips. Lighting it, he took a drag before releasing the smoke and watching it as it wafted upwards in the still afternoon air. "In a word: no. Jacob loves his bloody reign more than anything. I think it's an addiction at this point. The warm and loving parts of Jacob died long ago."

"But won't he just bring his brother back to life?"

"He will. It's the loss of honor that bothers him the most. He also knows the pain and suffering his brother will endure. Not only will Bobby remember the pain of his own death, but he will also have to endure the pain of the rebirth."

I wasn't sure how to respond, so I just stared for a moment. Momma's eerie prediction filled every space between each of the words Ben had spoken. As much as I dreaded the truth I recognized Ben's warning. "I don't feel too damned good about it, I can tell you that," I responded. "Boy fuckin' howdy, I wish I had never stopped for that Yoohoo!"

Ben produced another cigarette and lit it. Taking a quick drag, he savored the smoke for a moment and released it. I don't know what it is, but smoking seemed like some sort of communion whenever he did it. "Not stopping for that Yoohoo wouldn't have changed a thing. It all started when you were here in another life, and it is a part of something that is still within you today. These things are beyond the grasp of most mortal men, for immortality is understood only by those living within the realm of Wakan Tanka, the Great Spirit.

"The Great Spirit is something of which all of us are a part. When we are too focused on the material plane we lose our grasp of the beyond, the source of true existence. If we could only see that we are all one great family, realize that race, religion, gender, allegiances, and surnames are only material markers, and that we are all seeking in the same manner."

"I can't believe you're telling me this, Ben. I had those same thoughts a few minutes ago."

"You have made my point. We are all part of and in tune with the Great Spirit, but we build egos and forget where we came from.

We're all fools, Brady, every damn one of us. Seems to me we can't go back, but maybe if we could forgive we could finally go forward."

I watched Ben as his words trailed off and he quietly smoked his cigarette, his gaze suddenly focused on the distant horizon. "What we do in life affects more than what we see. We are so petty and materialistic that most of us never understand the fluidity and permanence of spirit. And spirit, my friend, is more real than the world we think we see around us."

Overwhelmed by the depth of meaning behind Ben's words I sat pondering them for a long time. The sudden flood of information was overwhelming, and I remained unsure that I could define exactly what he meant. Ben was wise beyond my understanding and this shit was way too deep for a simple country boy like me. I reckoned I better wrap myself around it the best I can all the same.

We didn't speak for a long time. Ben smoked, and I just sat looking out at the horizon and the beautiful blue Texas sky.

"So you're saying these demons would have found me no matter what?"

"I believe so."

"Do you think they really showed up and killed those other people just to get to me?" I turned to look at him with a frown on my face. I still didn't want to believe that all those people had died because of me or because of something I had done in a life I couldn't even remember.

"No, they killed those people because they needed living material to transform into physical beings, and it is more than likely that those people were probably chosen for the same reasons they have for killing you. I suspect all of you have something in your past, or the pasts of your ancestors, that drew them to you."

"This is some wild shit." I shook my head in disbelief and stared at Ben.

Ben looked back at me through the smoke of his cigarette. "There is something else you need to know."

"Okay."

"I told you Jacob and his Dancers have been to Texas before."

"Yeah, you mentioned it."

"In my discussion with Isatai I learned that Scar Lip, whose name in life was Kotsoteka, has risen before."

"Yeah, and?" I said unsure why this meant anything to me.

"You said your father abandoned you, and in a drunken stupor called and told you it was for your own protection. The truth is that he had an experience similar to yours, only he had no one to explain it to him. Isatai said your father saw a whirlwind rise and consume a fellow worker while rough-necking on an oil rig down near Seagraves.

"He knew the story because Kotsoteka visited him during that time. Your father had no idea what he was up against and did the only thing he thought he could do: hide from it and drink away the memory. It wasn't long before Kotsoteka found him anyway. He probably gave you a few extra years because his last act before dying was shooting down the man who killed him."

My mouth fell agape, and I sat stunned. My hatred for Scar Lip burned deeper while feelings about my father evolved to those of remorse and respect. I had always thought he abandoned me for his own selfishness, and now it seemed he had done so in order to keep me safe just like he'd said. I sat speechless stunned by this development. My father was far nobler than I ever thought possible.

"Mr. Drake."

The voice snapped me from my thoughts, and I turned to look at Agent Winters as she approached me, walking alongside the house. "Yes, ma'am?"

"Detective," she acknowledged Ben. "Would the two of you mind joining us for a little strategy session?"

Swift stood and followed me as I ventured in the direction of the others. Agent Winters reclaimed her seat at the octagonal shaped picnic table where agents, O'Reilly, and Nielsen continued to chat. I sat down to face them, and Ben sat in a lawn chair just to my left.

"It seems we may be wasting our time here," O'Reilly proclaimed. "We have new information that this gang of killers is striking all over this county. Knowing how mobile they've been in the past we think they may be moving on. It may be they've lost interest here after the confrontation in the pit. I'm considering moving my operation back to Lubbock."

"That doesn't make any sense to me, O'Reilly. They're still here in the area. Jacob Dark Moon is building an army; that's my take on this. He's responding to the confrontation at the pit not by 'moving on' but by bolstering his forces. I have little doubt he'll return here, and we best be ready when he does." Ben's face was set in a scowl as he addressed O'Reilly.

"You know some of these killers?" Agent Nielsen asked. "I mean you're calling them by name. I don't recall any names in the files."

"I know their names," Ben replied, unwilling to give more information than necessary.

"You've never mentioned names before, Ben." O'Reilly had a puzzled look on his face.

"Well if you know their names why don't we have files on them?" Nielsen pressured. He looked to the others for assistance when Swift failed to respond.

"Now, Ben, we have no individual files on these men. We've checked numerous police files, even your files in Pine Ridge, and there are no personal profiles on file anywhere," O'Reilly said. "The agency hasn't been able to determine exactly what it is we're dealing with; the criminal profiles we're using as a reference may not be accurate. If you can provide us with names and backgrounds for these individuals we need you to come clean with us."

"Other than running back to Lubbock what other strategies have you come up with?" Swift asked, ignoring questions about the Dancers' identities. He took a final drag off the stub of his cigarette before crushing it into the dirt beneath his shoe.

Both agents O'Reilly and Nielsen stared blankly at Ben, perplexed that he was not answering their questions.

"We feel strongly that we need to coordinate a dragnet with local and county police, covering what has now become a tri-county area." Agent Winters broke the uneasy silence. "This will mean roadblocks and quick response teams as well as an increase in patrols."

Swift," Agent Nielsen interjected, "it amazes me that this gang of killers has managed to avoid capture for so long. Especially when you seem to know them intimately. What could be so important? What possible motive could you have for not providing us with all that you know?"

Ben's eyes burned with resentment as he scowled at Agent Nielsen, who looked away. "Are you accusing me of being an accomplice to these men?" Ben's voice was eerie.

"I'm saying you seem to know a lot about them, yet you can't provide us with any information other than assisting in a generic profile. You know their names. None of us has ever heard the name Jacob Dark Moon. You may not be an accomplice, but you're certainly not being forthcoming. *That's* what I'm saying," Agent Nielsen replied.

Ben leaned forward and slammed his fist onto the bench seat of the picnic table. "I've tried to tell you Feds what I know, and you pompous assholes have passed it off as Indian mumbo-jumbo. 'The redskins telling spirit tales,' was what one of your field supervisors told the last agent I worked with. And that agent is now dead which is more than likely where you people are going to end up if you don't start listening. Forthcoming? You people have no ears! You arrogant bastards refuse to listen." With that, Ben spun on his heels and strode off across the sunburned lawn to disappear around the corner of the house.

"Damn, is he always that hot-headed?"

"Look, Scott, he's been at this for a while, and I'm sure not being able to catch these bastards has gotten to him. What we need to do now is focus on the best course of action and get these men before they kill or injure anyone else," Agent Winters explained.

"And you'll do that by remaining right here because I can *guarantee* you they'll be back." Ben returned with his jacket in hand and a fresh cigarette protruding from his lips.

"Why is that, detective? *Why* will they return here?" Nielsen scowled at Ben, his eyes dark.

"Because, as I continue to tell you, they want to kill Brady, and because they know I'm here. Try and remember that I've encountered these killers before. I strongly recommend you hang on a few more days because I believe you'll get your chance to engage these sons of bitches."

No one said anything for several minutes. Ben lit his cigarette while O'Reilly took a cell phone call, to which he listened more than spoke, and when it was over he glanced at the detective. "Okay, Ben, we'll give it two more days here. Do you have any recommendations as to how to capture these men?"

"First, you people must assume I'm right and that the men you are likely to encounter are the men doing the killing, but not the men you really seek. The most important thing we can do is to capture some of these killers and get them to lead us to Jacob. The problem is they are difficult to capture because they are so bent on killing, and have no value for their own lives. Unless we can disarm them or net them we aren't likely to capture any of them. With them it's kill or be killed.

"If we can get enough law officers in place we might get the upper hand. The safest and most reliable way to capture the Dancers is to mobilize enough choppers and personnel to hunt them openly. You've been promised the use of at least one chopper sometime within the next day or so. In the meantime, Winters, you and Nielsen should coordinate the dragnet with local and county law enforcement."

The others didn't seem too inclined to argue with Ben, and they quieted after that. It wasn't long before the silent, but unanimous, decision was made to go our separate ways. Once our little meeting adjourned I invited the detective to accompany me to Benny's for a quick cold one while the agents coordinated their dragnet. I never gave it a thought that I was bringing a police officer into a bootlegger's house. I'd grown accustomed to his laid back nature and considered him a friend, so it seemed natural. Benny gave me some funny looks on seeing the detective's badge displayed from where it was clipped on his belt, but we slugged down a couple of beers and left the place without incident.

But for watching a couple of agents arrive from Lubbock and then leave again, nothing else happened this evening. And I'm glad of that because it'd been several unbelievable days, and I'd seen and heard more than I can even begin to understand. Right now I just wanted to sleep. My mother's words had not ceased to haunt me, and I had begun to wonder if it really was "too late." Only time will tell, I reckon. With little hope, I end today's entry.

❊ 15 ❊

The new day dawned following an uneventful night. I had little appetite for breakfast as I sat at the table poking a fork into my eggs. My thoughts were consumed with memories of my daddy and the hatred I felt for Scar Lip and Dark Moon. I don't remember much about my dad, but between bouts of imagining his horrific experience with the dust devils and his untimely death I mourned his loss and treasured the moments we had shared. Every time I looked in on Momma I wrestled with the idea of telling her why Daddy disappeared and how he died. But I was unsure whether it would matter to her now, and I couldn't bring myself to. She passed the morning sitting on her bed hugging her knees to her chest and staring out the window while rocking back and forth. No matter how many times I asked her how she was doing she didn't answer me; she just kept staring.

I wandered between the house and the FBI's mobile office as I tried to sate that restless feeling in my gut. Despite the endless reports coming in over the radio, neither the Dancers nor any of their spawn had been seen. It was as if they'd vanished. Ben, on the other hand, was easy to find seated as he was in the shade cleaning his weapons. I asked him if he had any clue as to where the Dancers might be or what they might be doing.

"Preparing for war," he said as he stared off into space. I stood there for a while waiting for anything further but eventually went back inside when nothing more was offered.

The morning sun rose higher in the sky and became torturous for anyone remaining in its sizzling glare. Despite the heat the FBI agents went about their duties. Agent Winters, Sheriff Baker, Constable Wharem, Sergeant Dickens, and several officers from the Levelland police force spent the afternoon in the air-conditioned tactical trailer plotting and deciphering data gathered by the ongoing dragnet.

Anxious and bored, I sat in the living room looking out at the small town I've called home my entire life. I tried to pass the time by skipping through the channels on the television Eddie had loaned us, but the channel surfing soon became intolerable. Turning it off, I tossed the remote on the table and stared out the window. Despite what Ben had told me I still regretted stopping for that Yoohoo. I wished I'd never gone near the Morales' place, and I wished I had never hated the memory of my father.

And that poor girl, the one taken at Ten Mile Fork, and my father, and all the others for that matter, where have their spirits gone?

"Damn," I said aloud, as frustration overwhelmed me, "where the hell is all this bullshit coming from?"

"What bullshit is that?" J.J asked as he stepped inside the back door and made his way across the kitchen.

"Hey, J.J., damn it's good to see a friendly face," I said, rising from the chair I'd been planted in for the past two hours. For the first time in days I felt a smile on my face. "Just some philosophical bullshit that I conjured up from somewhere. It's all way too serious for a couple of truck-driving Texas boys, I reckon."

"Seems to me you got some right serious folks out there in the yard." J.J. ignored my answer. "Hell, I thought the police were going to strip search me on my way in here. And them in that fancy trailer out there. What damned government agency do they work for?"

"FBI."

"FBI! Damn, ain't this the shit?" he said, lifting his eyebrows in mock surprise. "I'd seen that trailer and all that shit out here, but I didn't know. Thought maybe they'd taken you away and were doing some kind of C.S.I. shit on your place."

"No, they think the killers are going to show up here. Some wild shit for sure. You want a beer or something?"

"Yeah, got any Lone Star?"

"I picked up some last night. I reckon there ought to be a few left in the fridge. Give me a minute."

"You heard from Billy Don?" J.J. asked as I pulled two bottles of beer from the refrigerator.

"No. How's he doing?"

"Ah, you know, same old Billy Don. But I know he ain't right with this whole thing. He's been pulling some of your weight, but he don't let nobody drive your rig. Hell, he ain't even let anyone go near it. The body shop fixed it up right as rain though and it looks good as new."

"Yeah, Skip always does nice work."

"You've taken to wearing a gun?"

"Yeah," I said, looking down at the Colt .45 revolver strapped to my right thigh. "So, ole Billy has been runnin' hard has he?"

"Yeah. Well, he's been doin' more than he likes let's just say that. He don't stay as long as he used to at the Cactus Creek after work. And sometimes he's in his rig well before dawn, so he don't make it into the diner for breakfast as regular as he use to either. Red says it's cause he's worrying about you, but Billy won't even talk about ya. Oh, by the way, the other guys said to tell you 'howdy', so you can consider that done."

"Jay, I'm damn glad you came by. Things have been way too serious around here. The bastards causing the trouble ain't somethin' to be joking about, but it's good to have somebody to talk to besides the cops and the feds."

"I have to admit it's hard to believe this story about dust devils and all. I reckon it's something you'd have to see with your own eyes to believe. I don't think Red or Billy believe a word of it, and well…" he paused, finding it hard to decide whether or not he believed it. "But I guess it's got to be true. Sure as hell, though, you're obviously dealing with some nasty pieces of work. So, what the hell is goin' on now, Brady? They gonna catch these guys, so you can come back to work?"

"You ain't going to believe it," I began, and spent the next few hours telling him the whole story as I know it. Around six o'clock we decided we'd drunk more than enough alcohol and needed to eat. I rooted around in the kitchen until I located some frozen hamburger patties, a bag of buns, pickles and potato chips, and we headed out to the picnic table where I fired up the gas grill. About half an hour later J.J., Ben, and I sat down to eat.

I barely noticed the sound of a cell phone ringing and someone out in front of the house answering it. Seconds later Agent Winters made her way into the back yard, looking tense and businesslike. "Detective, there's a raucous up at the convenience store alongside the highway. Somebody claims they've sighted a half naked Indian with a rifle running around. Local police are en route, and we're responding. You need to come now, if you care to join us."

Ben said nothing. He simply waved her off and took a long swig on the last bottle of Lone Star. Agent Winters gave me a quick glance before she turned and jogged toward the front yard. I looked at Ben wondering what I should do. Following his lead I returned to eating my supper despite being uncertain why he was cavalier about the situation. Somewhere in the distance a siren wailed as it approached town.

The sun disappeared behind the rolling bevy of dark clouds filling the sky to the south and west as we finished dinner. I saw Ben's head tilt to one side as though he was hearing something I didn't. Then I heard the faint and distant rumble of thunder and caught a slight chill. The ripple of electricity from the storm caused the hair to stand up on the back of my neck. A breeze began to blow, and all three of us watched as a small whirlwind kicked up the dust and spun for a moment just west of the table.

"Get inside," Ben said, standing and drawing his weapon as he moved toward the house. His tone was stoic and calm, but I knew it wasn't a suggestion.

"What's goin' on?" J.J. grabbed up his bottle of beer as he took one step away from the table before reaching back. He snagged a handful of potato chips before moving toward the back door to the house. My heart stopped as a twister began to encircle one of his legs. Leaping in his direction, I grabbed him by the arm and jerked him toward the house.

"Damn, Brady, I'm comin'," he whined as I released my grip on him. Turning to look around I noticed several more whirlwinds kicking up the dust. My hand fell to my sidearm as I looked about and followed the other two men inside.

"They're coming, aren't they," Momma called from her bedroom as the three of us filed into the living room. "I love you, Brady," she said in an oddly melancholy tone.

I stepped into her room to find her seated at her dressing table powdering her face and still wearing her nightgown. Striding across the floor to where she sat I kissed the top of her head lovingly. "You stay in here Momma, we'll take care of it."

Turning on my heel, I walked back through the door and pulled it shut behind me. As it closed to within an inch of the sill I heard Momma speak again. "I'll see you in heaven."

That freaked me right out, but I didn't have time to debate her, especially in her condition and with who-knows-what on the way.

Journal entry: September 06, 10:09 p.m. Heaven and hell have converged.

❊ 16 ❊

Holy shit. Look!" J.J. exclaimed, "Who the fuck are they?" Crushing my pen into the journal page, I lunged from chair and burst into the living room. J.J. was standing before the large plate glass window and pointing toward the old service station. Across the street, jogging across the open field and still about two hundred yards away, over two-dozen painted warriors moved as one.

Reaching for the gun rack above the fireplace I yanked a weapon off the wall and grabbed some ammunition from the shelf below. "Load it up," I said as I handed him a twelve gauge shotgun, a full box of slugs, and a belt holding two-dozen buckshot shells. I spun around dashed into my bedroom and gathered up as many weapons and boxes of ammunition as I could carry. Returning to the living room, I piled everything in one corner. I drew the Colt and made sure it was loaded and ready before returning it to the holster.

"What do I do with this?" J.J. asked, still standing as I had left him with the shotgun in one hand, ammo in the other, and a look of fear in his eyes.

"Don't think about it, J.J., just shoot these bastards 'cause if you don't they'll kill you." As I spoke I grabbed the Remington and shoved a few more rounds into the magazine.

"I can't," J.J. responded. His face was pale and his eyes were wide. I recognized the look and knew how he must be feeling.

"Look, I'm sorry, but you've got no choice in the matter. Either you help us or you die. You got that?"

"I can't, Brady! Hell, I ain't never killed nobody."

"You can—you've killed deer. It's just like killing deer. The only difference being is these fuckers will kill you if you don't kill them first. Now for your own sake, J.J., load that damn shotgun, and just do this!"

J.J. nodded a couple times, and I could see his throat convulse as he swallowed. He reluctantly loaded the shotgun as he looked nervously out through the window at the approaching warriors. Despite my own misgivings I could see he needed a little more reassurance.

"It's going to be all right," I said. "Just aim and squeeze. We'll get through this."

Just before the painted devils reached the service station on the other side of the street a black Chevy Suburban burst into the yard, and Agents Winters, Nielsen, and O'Reilly piled out of it. I reckoned they somehow missed seeing the warriors because they paid them no mind.

One of the approaching Indians fired, and his first bullet struck the Suburban. Then a second warrior fired, and his bullet also struck the vehicle and ricocheted wildly. I listened as it whined over the lawn and slammed into the roof of my house.

All three agents crouched down in unison and drew their weapons. O'Reilly called out, identifying himself as a federal agent, and fired a warning shot overhead. The tiny mob of warriors broke into a howl and charged the trio firing as they rushed forward. All three agents returned fire as they backed away and retreated toward the house.

Excited by the Agent's gunfire the warriors sprinted toward the house and began taking better aim. Agent Nielsen caught a bullet in the thigh and stumbled as a second shot ripped into the left side of his chest. I ducked as the front of my house was riddled with bullets and watched in horror as the swarm of angry demons entered the front yard. The bloodthirsty mob moved as one, firing rifles and swinging war clubs, all the while howling out war cries that stirred primitive emotions deep within me.

Sliding open one of the sidelight windows, I lay my rifle across the top of the sill and began to return fire. Ben, too, responded and wrenched open the front door, a Glock in each hand, and began firing at the oncoming horde. Between shots I marveled at his fearlessness as he stepped through the door and onto the front porch.

While O'Reilly continued to fire on the charging warriors with deadly accuracy, Agent Winters dropped to a crouch and moved to assist the fallen Nielsen.

Just as the she was about to reach Nielsen a whirlwind sprang up from the dirt and engulfed the wounded man. Fear and amazement swept across Agent Nielsen's face as he was lifted up and spun around as though he were nothing more than a rag doll. He managed a hideous scream as he was twisted violently and consumed by the dust-laden air.

Stumbling backward Agent Winters stared in fear and disbelief. When the twisting mass moved toward her she reflexively leaped away and barely escaped being sucked into the gurgling, snapping tempest.

"What the hell!" J.J. hollered as the whirlwind dissipated, and a naked warrior stumbled out of the dust. Agent Winters emptied her weapon into the warrior at point blank range, and it fell dead to the earth. I could see the shock and confusion on her face as she tried to process what had just happened.

"What the hell!" J.J. repeated. "Lord God in heaven, did you just see that?" Now he was screaming. "Brady, my God, Brady, it's true! It's really fuckin' true! Oh my fuckin' word!"

"For heaven's sake, J.J., I been tellin' ya…"

When Agents O'Reilly and Winters dashed around the corner to the rear of the house the front window shattered under the force of at least a dozen bullets as the warriors focused their firepower on Ben and me.

Ben, who had been providing the agents with cover fire from a tenuous position on the front porch, plunged backwards through the front door. Tumbling across the floor in one fluid motion he reloaded as he struggled to his feet and immediately continued returning fire from a half-crouched position. I'd never seen anyone fight like Ben could, but I figured with how long he'd been around it made sense.

J.J. and I instinctively dropped to the floor.

Feeling a searing burn in my side and face I glanced at the bloody crease along the left side of my rib cage. I pulled up my shirt and plucked several large shards of glass from my flesh. As I brushed more shards from my face I peered over the sill and fired until my weapon was empty before I ducked down and reloaded.

"I think I'm hit," J.J. yelped, his bloody hand drawing away from a hole in his shirt just below the shoulder.

"You're okay, J.J., you're okay," I assured him. "Just a flesh wound. But I need your help. Just aim that shotgun and pull the trigger!" I peeked my head up again and fired once more through the opening in the partially shattered glass of the front window. I heard a crashing sound in the kitchen and glanced in that direction. "Shoot anything that moves!" I barked toward J.J. before running toward the back door, weapon at the ready, only to see O'Reilly and Agent Winters stumble inside.

Winters slammed the door shut and locked the knob as bullets destroyed the glass above where she squatted. I looked her over to see if she was hurt anywhere and noticed that blood soaked a small portion of the back of her white blouse. She winced as she fell to her knees, and as she lifted her face our eyes met for just a moment. Whatever she saw there she nodded once before speaking up. "I'll cover this!" she bellowed and returned fire into the darkening gloom outside.

O'Reilly and I made our way into the living room where Ben and J.J. were firing relentlessly. As a half dozen warriors leaped up onto the porch I aimed my Remington and gunned down one after the other until the weapon was empty. Off somewhere towards the center of town I could hear sirens wailing as they approached.

Reinforcements? God, I hoped so.

I will never forget the shrill scream that rang out next. With dread in my heart I lunged for the door to my mother's bedroom. I drew my pistol with one hand while fumbling the knob with the other. I managed to unlatch the door and burst into the room. The sight of the bloody knife withdrawing from my mother's navel sickened me, and pain gripped my heart. A sense of failure and loss punched me with the force of a professional boxer, and I stood transfixed as I stared helplessly at her body. My Momma dangled in mid-air suspended by her hair which was clenched in the fist of a large, gruesome-looking warrior.

The man was standing in the middle of the room, his naked flesh covered head to toe in paint, and with an aura of pure malice emanating from his entire being he prepared to drive the knife into my mother again. Aiming at his smirking face I pulled the trigger again and again, shattering his skull as though it were a ripe melon and riddling his dancing corpse as it stumbled and pivoted backward, releasing the limp body of my mother as it did so.

As the dead Comanche fell through the gaping hole that once housed the window I lunged to grab my mother.

Bullets punched holes through the house, whining loudly as they sliced past me and plowed into the walls. Squatting down, I lifted my mother and made my way to her bed. I laid her gently atop the bedspread and brushed the long, flowing hair back from her eyes. Tears rolled down my cheeks as my heart squeezed with emotion.

"Brady, Brady," she whispered.

Thinking she was already dead, I wrapped my arms around her. Lifting her slightly from the mattress and pulling her to me, I kissed her on the face. "Momma, oh Momma, I'm so sorry."

"Brady, finish your journal… Warn others," she gasped as blood trickled from her quivering lips. As her body shook she whispered, "It's beautiful, Brady. I see Roger, I…" With that she released her last breath, and her body relaxed. In that moment I knew she was gone.

Tears flowing from my eyes I buried my face in her chest and eased her body to the mattress. I sobbed even as fury rose within me. Only the sense that someone was approaching wrenched me from my sorrow. Looking up, my eyes met those of a warrior just entering the opening in the wall. I raised my revolver and pulled the trigger. The click of the hammer on an empty chamber echoed through my head like thunder. By the time I realized the implications of the sound the charging warrior was already on me.

We rolled from the impact, but my hand managed to grasp the wrist of his right hand, which held a large, serrated knife. As we struggled with one another his large, black eyes glared at me. His breath smelled like a corpse, and drool spilled from his lips onto my face.

Two gunshots rang out, and the demon collapsed. Scooting out from under the naked corpse, I turned to look at my savior. There in the doorway stood Eddie Wharem clad in a white t-shirt beneath his unbuttoned Constable uniform. Bleeding from the neck, the left shoulder, and the right side of his abdomen, he glared down the barrel of his smoking .44 magnum revolver.

"You okay, Brady?" he grunted.

"T-thanks, Eddie," I stammered as I pushed myself to my feet. I quickly noted the pallor of his skin. "You've been hit."

"Yeah, stinkin' Indians got me." We both squatted down behind the bed, avoiding the stray bullets raking the walls of the room, "Then Agent Winters mistook me for one of them when I tried the back door. Shot me right here," he said, angling his weapon to point at the hole in his lower left abdomen. "Reckon I'll live. A bit longer anyway. Looks like the nightmare you've been telling everyone about has come true."

"Yeah, Eddie, and I reckon the shit is fixin' to get worse. A lot worse."

"Sorry about your mother." He nodded toward the bed. I reloaded my weapon with shaking hands. A dozen more holes appeared in the wall above our heads, and plaster rained down onto both of us.

"Bastards," Eddie grumbled. He leaped up and charged toward the window, firing as he did so. As Eddie found cover to the left of the gaping hole his bullets struck down several warriors as they approached the opening. Following him, I leaped to the other side of the opening and peered outside. The sky had darkened, and lightning shattered the storm-laden clouds above as a fierce wind thrashed the foliage in the trees to my right. The front yard and street were illuminated by a half-dozen squad cars of various law enforcement agencies, all of them having converged on my tiny house. Blue and red lights flashed like beacons at an amusement park while lawmen engaged the Comanche warriors.

As I pumped lead into two warriors charging the house I was stunned to see Sheriff Baker engrossed in a fierce battle, a pistol in each hand, and surrounded by a fierce mob. In that moment I felt a certain bond with the man though I lost sight of him as he disappeared into the fray.

Everything seemed incredibly odd to me in those few moments, and I saw things with a clarity I don't remember ever experiencing before. The attacking Indians seemed oddly familiar, like I had been here before, and the chaos seemed to have some rhythmic flow as though it were being orchestrated in some strange way. For a moment I visualized an evil maestro, a devilish fiend of universal proportion, waving his wand and sending wave after wave of vengeful spirits toward my home, all of whom seemed to be dancing to the rhythms of the Dancer's drum. At the last few seconds of the vision I pictured that maestro to be me.

Snapping back to reality I noticed that, strangely enough, some of the policemen were firing on the house while others battled the real enemy.

Whirlwinds spinning up out of the Texas dust were engulfing police officers as they arrived on the scene and left their vehicles. I realized with horror the ranks of our enemies were growing from amongst those arriving to save us. Born in me at that moment was the fear that all was truly lost.

"Sorry to leave you, Eddie, but I got something I need to do."

"Go on, Brady. I'll see you in hell," Eddie stated soundly while reloading his revolver. With a smirk and a wink he struggled to portray an aura of bravado then turned away and began firing once more into the swarm of attackers.

"I'll be back."

Driven by my mother's final request, I stumbled into my bedroom. The immediate horror of seeing the journal missing from my desk caused me to sink further into the gloom of despair. I dropped to my knees and frantically searched amongst the books and papers scattered about the floor. The pain of my wounds crept into my awareness as I spotted a corner of the open journal protruding from beneath a dirty shirt. Pulling the pen from the binding of the book I placed it on the desk and began jotting down these final words.

This will be my final entry. Sacred is the circle for, like the energy of the spirit, it appears to be without end.

✳ **17** ✳

I am resolved to complete something I hope will be meaningful. In the few minutes I have taken to make this final entry I fear my friends suffer for my absence. The fighting has intensified, and I don't think we'll be coming out of this alive.

I'm thinkin' I can take enough of these dust devils along with me to make a difference. I don't know if this makes sense. I've lost a fair bit of blood and might not be thinkin' straight. The house is shaking, and it sounds like a freight train is passing nearby. I'm going to stuff this in the box I prepared for mailing. It has your address, and I hope it reaches you. Maybe you can warn others. Maybe you can see life as something larger, and act as though each moment impacts you for eternity. I wish I had, but I didn't know then what I know now. Life is funny that way. Seems like by the time you learn enough to make things right you've already made them wrong enough that there ain't no fixin' it. I pray it's not too late for my soul.

Letter from a Stranger

Dear Stranger,   September 9th…

By now you've received a parcel. You have likely read the letter, and maybe you've leafed through parts of the journal. I am sorry to inform you that Brady's death is quite literal. He did not survive the attack on his home. His mother has also met with an untimely end, and so I send along my condolences for your loss.

Although you and I may never meet it is apparent to me that you are someone Brady trusted and, I hope, someone who will take the knowledge we are sending you and use it to inform others.

I would like to continue in that tradition. Brady's efforts to keep a journal have inspired me to do the same. I realize the difficulties you face. Foremost is in accepting what we have written and in revealing the contents of these journals to anyone else.

Enclosed is the beginning of my own journal. Being that I am on the move I feel that my words will be safer with you than they are with me. In these writings are the final moments of your friend, and matters relevant to this moment. Know that my crossing between this reality and the spirit world allows me glimpses of occurrences I would never see otherwise.

I hope to expose the Shadow Dance and provide some insight into the spirit world in general. I will continue to send along my journals as they are completed unless I hear otherwise from you. My life will end one day, most likely in a violent act, but as long as I breathe I will pursue Jacob Dark Moon.

Remember, we are all connected. Go and tell this story, and share the words in the journals yet to come. Knowing that we are immortal and that what we have done in the past and what we do now—in this lifetime—impacts each of us for eternity is a message not only of hope but a warning.

Sincerely,
Ben Swift,
Detective, Pine Ridge Police

❋ 1 ❋

From the front door, where I fired into the swarm of specters rising from the dust in front of the Drake residence, I watched Brady return from the inner confines of the house.

Brady rushed into the living room with his journal tucked firmly beneath one arm. Diving to the floor he winced as pain exploded through his wounded body, and he lay still for a moment to recover. Brady struggled to creep forward, and I knew from the color of his face he'd lost too much blood. Plaster exploded from the walls as hundreds of tiny missiles ripped through the structure. They must have begun using fire arrows because moments later the walls erupted in flame and folded like paper while the few brave souls inside the house scrambled along the floor and tried to continue the fight.

Brady crawled to the front of the house and pulled himself into a seated position leaning back against the wall under the front window in a relatively clear spot. Between shots I kept an eye on him as he spotted a piece of paper and pencil on the floor nearby. Brady scribbled something on the surface and slipped it inside the cover of the journal. Shaking loose the pencil, his fingers struggling to cooperate with his intentions, Brady managed to stuff the journal into the addressed and post-marked box I remembered seeing him prepare days earlier.

Above him his friend J.J. continued to fire at the enemy. I knew in the pit of my stomach that both men weren't long for the world. I'd seen this too many times before to not recognize the creeping grip of death.

Sealing the box Brady glanced upward as O'Reilly stumbled through the door from the nearby bedroom and fell heavily to the living room floor. His pistol gripped securely in one hand the severely wounded,

Agent O'Reilly wriggled across the floor leaving a trail of blood staining the wood behind him. Two feet from where Brady sat O'Reilly was unable to crawl any further. In an incredible feat of strength he lifted his head until his eyes met Brady's. "You were right," he gurgled before his bloody, lifeless head struck the hardwood floor.

Staring at the dead man, Brady seemed removed as he tossed the sealed parcel aside and ducked reflexively in response to another volley of bullets. The man struggled to his feet, pistol in hand, and emptied the weapon towards the growing threat outside while ignoring the bullets whizzing past him and through him. They slammed into the walls beneath and behind the man's feet, and one grazed his skull. Finally, Brady slumped to the floor, leaned forward, and patted his friend on the shoulder.

J.J. huddled down next to him struggling to reload his shotgun. Every act was a determined challenge for their exhausted bodies, and I saw J.J.'s hands trembling.

"I'm sorry, Jimmy," gasped Brady.

"Ah, fuck it," J.J. panted as his hollow gaze focused on Brady and tears streamed down his face. "I just hope my Felicia is okay." Staring for just a moment longer, he focused once more on the task at hand. Brady looked up and called out to his friend, Eddie. I'm sure he worried for him and wanted to know whether he was dead or if he had become one of the *unwakanpi.*

Brady's head swung back and forth as he struggled to focus. I knew how he felt. When you're dying everything moves in a surreal sense of time with each moment disconnected from the one before. I saw those things in Brady Drake now, and with one last glance at the parcel he reached for the handgun in O'Reilly's outstretched hand. Brady wrenched the weapon free and forced himself to his feet. Clenching a pistol in each of his hands he fired at the swarm of *unwakanpi* battling their way toward the house.

More bullets ripped through Brady's flesh, twisting his body, and he was knocked to the floor. His left hand, bloody and crippled, struck the package he had just prepared. He had no more will to rise, and was no longer capable of fighting.

"It sounds like a freight train comin'," Brady gasped at J.J.

"Maybe it's the train to heaven coming, Brady," J.J. replied through blood-drenched lips. Plaster cracked around us, and the walls creaked as they bowed inward wildly. It was no freight train that we heard. The air around the house became alive with debris being hurled about by the hands of the sky as the tornado wrapped itself around all of us.

Brady glanced upward as something passed through the window above him with a look of serenity on his face. Fear had left him moments ago, just as it had left me, and he basked in a sense of release as he recognized the bloody and wounded form of Scar Lip looming over him. "I guess you finally have me."

"As you once had me," growled the warrior who then fell upon him. The knife blade flashed, and as Brady fought through the initial pain he sought the eyes of his destroyer.

"Momma," he called out. The tone of wonder in his voice filled me. Staring into the dark wrathful eyes of the man he had deemed Scar Lip, Brady suffered yet another thrust of the angry blade.

I cannot explain this in any way that will make sense, but in that final moment I shared a vision with Brady Drake. In an action I think is one of the most noble I've ever seen, I could hear him asking God for forgiveness for both their souls.

"Please forgive me, as I forgive you now," Brady groaned through clenched teeth, his eyes staring into those of his enemy. I could only watch in awe as the other man's eyes transformed, becoming normal. I sensed brotherhood between them, a moment of knowing that they were one with the other. As their bodies fell their spirits fled them in unison to return to the spirit world. I felt myself smile as I saw peace come to both of them, and as the tornado around us drew the house, the *unwakanpi,* and the remnants of the police upwards into the sky I thanked the Great Spirit.

Epilogue

Television anchor teams interrupted late night television shows across the country, spreading the news about an incredibly powerful tornado that wiped the small town of Broken Spoke, Texas, off the map.

Rescue workers arriving on the scene in the wee hours of the morning were sickened by the utter devastation of what they believed had to be a larger and more powerful tornado than any class F5 yet recorded. Nothing remained of the town but for a few smoldering walls and the concrete slabs where the school, the convenience store, and three-dozen houses had been. Homes without concrete foundations left little evidence of their existence beyond bare patches of ground in the shape of squares or rectangles.

Reporters and authorities found no trace of the FBI agents or the more than four-dozen law enforcement officers who reportedly had descended upon the community. Official press releases on the matter first stated that the officers had been dispatched to Broken Spoke in response to a domestic dispute. However, they later changed the story to report that officers had actually been involved in the culmination of a hunt for a man suspected of arson and a series of murders.

"It's a tragic event that police responding to apprehend a suspected serial killer, a local man named Brady Drake, were caught in the tornado," one official was quoted as saying.

The 'violent and destructive' twister had touched down just west of the small town, and strangely dissipated less than half a mile east of the ravaged community. The mangled bodies of only a few of the town's inhabitants were found, and debris, including the many police vehicles, was strewn for miles in all directions. Search efforts over the following days yielded neither survivors nor any other corpses, although clothing, appliances and other debris was discovered as far away as fifty miles.

The town of Broken Spoke, Texas, existed no more.

And just a few miles northwest of the remnants of Broken Spoke, in the town of Whiteface, Texas, a young girl playing a game of tag with several of her schoolmates darted along the street on her way to school. Suddenly, she spotted a parcel lying on the sidewalk only a few feet from a blue metal U.S. Post Office mailbox. "Hey look," she shouted cheerfully.

Immediately breaking into a run she raced several of her nearby friends to the thin rectangular package. She giggled as she snatched up the parcel while dodging the grasp of one of her classmates. Glancing down at her newfound prize she noticed a sticky, red stain on the brown corrugated packaging next to the mailing label. "Yuck!"

"Where's it from?" asked one of the other girls.

"Broken Spoke. Someone must have meant to mail it and missed the mailbox."

"Maybe the mailman dropped it," offered one of the other girls.

"Maybe."

"Hey, that's not yours. Leave it alone," her older brother scolded as he and several other boys his age approached her. "Give it to me."

"It's not yours, either!" The girl's face drew up and she stuck her tongue out in his direction in an expression of childish defiance.

"It will be," he responded as he quickened his steps and moved directly toward her.

Before he could take it from her she flashed him a rebellious smile and opened the mailbox before tossing the package inside.

On that same morning, less than three miles away from the devastation and carnage of what was once the community of Broken Spoke, Rowley Jacobs stepped down from his tractor to inspect a pile of wreckage that had fallen from the sky and planted itself in the center of his cotton field. He had taken only ten steps from the idling machine when a whirling mass of sand arose from amongst the furrows of cotton shrubs and glided across the land directly toward him. Dodging the path of the oncoming dust devil he was startled when the whirlwind changed course and followed him. The wind intensified, and the twisting torrent engulfed his body. Rowley, amazed and then terrified, bellowed in protest as his body began to spin and pain wracked his entire being.

When the roaring twister subsided and began to dissipate Rowley Jacobs no longer existed. Instead the naked form, the ever evolving embodiment of Detective Benjamin Swift, stumbled from its wake. Ben collapsed to the soil and shuddered with pain from the transformation. Slowly, his body straightened, and he shook his aching head. He flinched as he shielded his eyes against the bright, morning sun and traced his fingers over the medicine bundle hanging from the sinew around his neck.

"Dark Moon, you bastard. Have you not tired of these foolish games?" he shouted.

Looking about and getting his bearings he searched momentarily for any sign of Brady and the others. Intuition told him they were gone, passed over to the other side, and he discovered nothing more than an endless field of cotton, an idling tractor, and the vast, blue Texas sky. Scanning the horizon, Ben spotted the sunlight glinting off vehicles as they traveled along a distant highway.

Ben quickly considered taking the tractor but immediately rejected the machine. The person he had replaced would soon be reported missing, and the less evidence linking him to the scene the better. Remorse for Jacob's endless games taking yet another life filled him as he turned away and began walking across the crop field. After a few unsteady and painful steps he found his stride and worked his way toward the road he had seen a moment before.

Spotting a patch of denim amongst the green cotton shrubs Ben stooped and snatched up the farmer's overalls. The left leg was sheared off at the knee, the other was frayed at the cuff, and one strap was gone. Again he considered the fact that the clothing might tie him to the farmer, but decided that it was safer to be clothed once he reached the road. Slipping into the tattered clothing he pulled the remaining strap over his shoulder and continued his journey. After taking several steps he checked the pockets and was pleasantly surprised to discover a cigarette pack in one of the buttoned pouches.

Ben fumbled with the lid to the Marlboro box and was relieved to find several cigarettes nestled alongside a chrome-plated butane lighter inside.

"Smoking. Yeah, it's a nasty habit, but what is it going to do, kill me?" he said aloud. His mouth twisted in a sarcastic grin that felt as ugly as it looked.

Placing a cigarette between his lips Ben flicked the lighter and inhaled gratefully before looking upward and releasing the smoke into the sky. As his head cleared, a multitude of thoughts subsided to allow Ben to form a clear and coherent message. As the smoke rose from his mouth Ben mumbled a solemn oath, "With the Great Spirit as my witness, I promise your days are numbered, and I pray they be few, Jacob Dark Moon. Let us die together, my brother, and be forever removed from our tortured path."

In silent resolve he walked through the waist-high cotton in the direction of the unknown. He knew in his guts that the wildfire of Jacob's wrathful indulgence would spread across the earth. And that he would continue to follow in its wake.

www.ingramcontent.com/pod-product-compliance
Lightning Source LLC
Chambersburg PA
CBHW071153180726
48291CB00007B/2442